OFFICE HOURS

M. Broughton Boone

Cape Winds Press, Inc.
2000

Printed in the United States of America on acid-free paper
First Edition

ISBN 0-9671203-4-9

Library of Congress Number: 00-190827

Published by Cape Winds Press, Inc.
P.O. Box 730428
Ormond Beach, FL 32173-0428
http://www.capewindspress.com

Cover design by Mary Boone incorporating images obtained from IMSI's MasterClips/MasterPhotos© Collection, 1895 Francisco Blvd. East, San Rafael, CA 94901-5506, USA

The breeze shifted direction and Kaitlan was again aware of the scent Cynthia wore as it drifted past her nose. It brought up a flash of desire so brilliant and sudden that Kaitlan took a physical step from the power of it.

Unfortunately, the step she took put her even closer to the source. Almost in Cynthia's arms, Kaitlan looked down at her and swallowed against the ache she felt.

"Kaitlan...." Cynthia's eyes were wide, but she made no attempt to move away. Kaitlan put her hands on Cynthia's shoulders and stared into her face.

"It would be so easy to fall into your eyes and drown," she said. "And I don't think I would fight at all."

Also By The Author

Not Me! I Scream
Poetry of Despair and Inner Peace
(Stone Hill Press)

Tahoma

About the Author

M. Broughton Boone lives with the loves of her life in Ormond Beach, Florida, on a small farm replete with a variety of animals. When she is not writing, she creates poetry and follows the stock market. Her other hobbies include boating, fishing, volleyball, golf, gardening, and watching the UNC Tarheels play basketball. You may contact her at M.Boone@capewindspress.com.

I.

With a sigh of relief, Kaitlan Davis guided her sleek black Saab 940 into a vacant spot in the employee parking lot of J. Jacobs, Inc. She had been snarled in traffic on I-5 for what seemed like hours, and was glad she had allowed herself extra time to get to work.

Adjusting the rear view mirror, she removed her sunglasses and checked her makeup once more. Satisfied, she ran long fingers through short, thick blonde hair and opened the door. A quick glance at her Timex showed that she was still half an hour early.

Good, she thought as she reached behind the seat for her briefcase, *at least I'll be able to impress the boss with my promptness.* She closed and locked the door and turned toward the low glass-walled building which housed her new employer. The early morning sun glinted off the mirrored glass, temporarily blinding Kaitlan, and she bent her head before starting to walk across the pavement.

1

It was a crisp winter morning, the blue sky something of a novelty to rain-weary Seattleites. Kaitlan pulled the lapels of her calf-length camel wool coat tighter around her throat as a gust of wind caught her off guard. She had left Spokane in two feet of snow, was grateful for the warmer climate of the Emerald City, but the wind here was enough to make her crazy. It never seemed to stop blowing.

Reaching the entrance to the building, Kaitlan stepped quickly through the double doors and out of the wind. She surveyed the lobby, and then turned to the security kiosk next to her - a concession to the military, she guessed, knowing that the company held several DoD contracts - and smiled at the uniformed man sitting there.

"Good morning. Could you direct me to personnel?"

"Down the corridor, third door on the left. You have to sign in, ma'am." He held up a clipboard with a pen attached by a chain. Kaitlan signed her name, hesitated a moment next to it, then filled in the spot for title with Senior Accounts Representative. The guard glanced at her name, and nodded.

"Thank you," Kaitlan said before walking off down the hallway looking for the third door on the left. She found it, and stepped into a cluttered office that seemed too small for the three desks crammed inside. There was a woman on the phone at the desk directly in front of her, and the other two desks were empty, so Kaitlan went and stood patiently by the woman.

She spoke for a few moments longer, then hung up

2

and gave Kaitlan the once over. "May I help you?"

"I'm Kaitlan Davis. The new accounts executive," Kaitlan added when the woman didn't appear to recognize her name. The woman at the desk, Carol, if her nameplate was to be believed, frowned.

"You're Ms. Davis? I was expecting someone a little - older." Kaitlan flushed. She knew she didn't look thirty-five, but it was embarrassing to be reminded of the fact.

"Yes," she said firmly. "I'm Ms. Davis."

"Ah. Well, welcome to J. Jacobs. I'm Carol, the personnel supervisor. Have a seat, won't you? There are a few forms I need you to fill out."

Five minutes later, with a Styrofoam cup of coffee sitting on the desk beside her, Kaitlan was filling out a stack of paperwork she hoped wasn't indicative of her new duties. There were personnel file forms, emergency notification forms, release forms, tax forms, life insurance forms, payroll forms.

Kaitlan paused when she came to the beneficiary line of her insurance form. She had been filling the form out automatically, and had almost written in Dana's name. It brought the same old familiar shock of pain to her chest to remember that Dana wasn't hers any more. She hadn't been for almost a year.

Sighing, Kaitlan put her mother and father on the line and went on with her paperwork. She wouldn't let Dana ruin her first day at work. It had been too long and the scars were too old.

She was glad she'd given herself the extra half hour by the time she was finished. Carol took the stack of papers away from her and glanced over them, then put them down on her desk and stood. "I'll show you to accounts," she said.

Kaitlan's department was all the way in the back of the building, next to the break room. It had its own lobby, complete with leather sofa and comfortable chairs and a receptionist with long blonde curls ensconced behind a large oak desk. The carpet was a forest green with a crème inlay, the walls painted white. Glass fronted offices opened off two sides of the room, the third wall, behind the receptionist, taken up by three solid doors.

The receptionist stood up when the two women came in. "This is Ms. Davis," Carol said smoothly, turning to indicate Kaitlan with her hand. "She's all yours."

The receptionist nodded. "Good. Welcome to accounts, Ms. Davis."

"Thank you." The nameplate on the desk read Megan Hobbs. "Thank you, Ms. Hobbs."

"Please, call me Meg. I'll show you to your office." Carol quietly slipped out of the room as Meg came around the desk. "Ms. Perry is in a meeting right now, but as soon as she's done she'll be out to give you your orientation. Would you like a cup of coffee or a latte?"

"You have an espresso machine?" Kaitlan glanced over at her and raised an eyebrow.

"Of course. You're in Seattle now, Ms. Davis. Our customers expect a certain level of sophistication."

Meg led Kaitlan to the door on the end of the wall, and showed her into a large office furnished with an oak desk, high back executive chair, bookcases, and two comfortable looking easy chairs. It was a corner room, and so two walls were completely glassed in, giving a view out over a green field and the stand of trees beyond.

"I'll take a latte, please," Kaitlan said to cover her surprise at the size of the office. She hadn't expected it to be so large. Meg nodded.

"Hazelnut, Irish Cream, Butterscotch, Jamaican Rum, Cinnamon, or Vanilla?"

"Cinnamon. Thank you, Meg." Meg went out, leaving Kaitlan standing in the middle of her new office.

There was already a nameplate on her desk with her name on it, heavy brass and shiny new. Kaitlan went over and ran her fingers lightly across the engraved letters.

This was a far cry from her small office space at Roreson's in Spokane. But Kaitlan had only been an accounts representative there. Here she was second in command to the Vice President of Accounts, a huge jump up the corporate ladder.

There was a light rap at the glass by her door and Kaitlan turned to see a tall, well-dressed African-American man standing outside. "May I come in?"

"Please."

He entered, hand outstretched. "I'm William Flint. You must be our new exec."

"Kaitlan Davis. Yes." She shook his hand.

"Most of the staff is in our Monday morning meeting, so you'll have to wait to meet them. I escaped by the grace of Janie." When Kaitlan looked confused, he grinned. "My daughter. She had an orthodontic appointment this morning, so I was able to slide out of the meeting. Trust me, you'll be glad for little miracles like that too, before too long. Cynthia's a tough nut."

Cynthia Perry, Kaitlan's boss. She wondered what Cynthia was like; she'd never worked for another woman before, and the prospect both excited her and made her nervous. "A tough nut?"

"She'll stand up to the most difficult customer, usually get them to go her way too. You'll see." He glanced at his watch. "Well, I guess I'm officially on company time now. Nice to meet you, Kaitlan."

Kaitlan leaned against her desk and watched him leave, then turned and took off her coat, hanging it on the brass coat tree in the corner. She smoothed the lines on her business suit, then went back to the desk and opened her briefcase.

Out of it she withdrew her diplomas and the photograph of her parents she kept on her desk. It was all she dared bring until she knew exactly what was allowed.

In Spokane, she had kept a picture of Dana on her desk, until Dana had moved to Arizona with the woman Kaitlan had thought to be her best friend. But Kaitlan had been out in Spokane. She didn't know what the climate was like at J. Jacobs.

She didn't have a girlfriend's picture to display anyway. She'd been celibate since Dana left. It was probably that which landed her this job; she'd spent so much extra time on her accounts that she'd won three major sales awards in the past six months alone.

Applying for the J. Jacobs position had been a flight of fancy. Kaitlan had wanted to get back to Seattle ever since Dana left, and when she had heard of the opening, she had wasted no time sending in her resume. She never expected to get the job, but apparently someone had been impressed enough to hire her.

So here she was. Now what? Kaitlan experienced a momentary panic; she'd been hired by mistake, she wasn't qualified to do this job....

"Here's your latte, Ms. Davis." Meg returned, balancing a large ceramic mug on top of a pile of file folders. "And the first of your accounts. I thought you'd like to get started while you wait for Ms. Perry."

"Thanks, Meg. And please, call me Kaitlan." Her moment of panic passed and Kaitlan tried to relax.

Meg frowned a little. "That would be against office policy. Didn't you get an employee handbook?" Kaitlan shook her head, mystified. The panic started to return and she forced it down. *I'm qualified for this position.* "I'll have to get you one. Carol must have forgotten to mail it to you."

"Thank you. Do you happen to have a hammer and a couple of nails?" She hoped it wasn't against office policy to hang things on the walls.

"Yes. I'll get them to you. The staff meeting should be over any time, so make yourself comfortable and Ms. Perry will come see you in a bit."

Kaitlan watched Meg leave, closing the door

behind her, then went and sat down in her chair and turned to look out the window. After a moment, she reached back and picked up her latte and the first file. Blowing gently on the mug, she took a sip and stared out the window at the field, the file unopened in her lap.

Dana had always hated Seattle, hated the wind and the rain and the cold. They had met at the University of Washington, where Kaitlan had been studying for her MBA and Dana had been in the graduate program for psychology.

Kaitlan had been immediately taken by Dana, tall and athletic. Their courtship was brief and passionate, and when the year was over and Dana graduated, planning to return to Spokane, Kaitlan was more than willing to go with her. She had postponed her schooling for three years before finishing at Washington State.

For twelve years she and Dana had been the model of a loving, committed lesbian couple. They owned a house together, had even spoken of having children. Then Kaitlan had come home to find her lover gone, to find that her own best friend was responsible, and that everyone who knew them had known about the affair, that is everyone except Kaitlan herself.

Dana and Rebecca were in Arizona and she was back in Seattle. And the pain felt like it would never go away. Kaitlan wondered if she would ever find another woman attractive again.

A sharp rap on the door interrupted her musings. "Come in!" Kaitlan swiveled around and put down her cup, then looked up at the newcomer and promptly forgot how to breathe.

Jet black hair, straight and thick, shoulder length, pulled back on each side with a cloisonné comb, green/brown eyes that sparked with intelligence, a long face evoking a Native American background, she was thin and small, and anywhere from thirty to forty-five.

Kaitlan's eyes traveled from a carefully made up face down a short slender neck to a sedate green linen business suit of a slightly lighter shade than the carpet, to full breasts, a slender waist, and down curving hips that flowed into firm-looking thighs and calves, to a pair of black pumps.

"I'm Cynthia Perry," the woman said, stepping into the office and closing the door firmly behind her. She extended a hand. "Welcome aboard, Kaitlan."

Kaitlan rose to shake hands. Cynthia's grip was measured, giving a hint of strength without exerting pressure. Her hands were small, the fingers long and elegant. Kaitlan took a deep breath and indicated a chair. "Please, sit down."

She was glad that Cynthia did, as it gave her an excuse to sink back down into her own seat. She was uncomfortably aware of the tiny ache that had started between her legs.

Cynthia smoothed her skirt, crossed her ankles, and leaned back, resting her hands on the arms of the chair. It was a pose that seemed calculated to indicate openness. "I apologize for not being available to meet you when you arrived. I didn't expect you to get done in personnel so quickly."

"I got here early," Kaitlan replied, feeling suddenly awkward, her eyes drawn to the fine gold chain that glittered, just barely visible, in the V of the crème silk blouse under Cynthia's jacket. It was hard to tell if the tone of her skin was natural or a tan. "I was just getting used to the office."

"That's fine. I'll arrange a tour of the facility for you after lunch. I glanced over your resume, very impressive. I hope you can be as successful with our clients as you were with Roreson's."

"I was under the impression that my position here was as more of a supervisor." Nervously, Kaitlan began to rub her hands along the arms of her chair. It was an old habit. Despite the calculated friendliness of her pose, Cynthia's self-assured professionalism bordered on conceit, and Kaitlan felt off balance.

"It is." Cynthia nodded. "But you'll still have some customer contact. You'll be overseeing six account reps in this office. If they have a problem, they come to you. If you can't handle it, you come to me. Think you can manage that?"

"Yes." Kaitlan swallowed hard and tried not to blush. She wondered what scent Cynthia was wearing. It was familiar, yet foreign and exotic. Cynthia's combination of femininity and steel nails was so distracting that Kaitlan felt like she was fresh out of the University of Washington again, nervously listening to her first job orientation.

"Remember, this is still a man's game. You don't look very far out of college, so you'll have to be tough to get the respect you need to do this job. But you can get it."

"I'm thirty-five. I know the score." She didn't know why she felt suddenly defensive, but she did. She had been working since graduating college at twenty-one, had gotten her MBA while still working. She knew quite well what the score was.

"I know how old you are. But you don't look it. I expect a lot out of my people, and I expect you to expect a lot out of them as well. How much do you know about what we do here?"

"J. Jacobs manufactures environmental control systems primarily designed for the aerospace industry." Kaitlan proceeded to list off a few of the facts she'd gleaned from the job description and from Dun and Bradstreet.

"Yes. We carry several large accounts with Boeing, as well as contracts with the Department of Defense. William Flint is our DoD specialist. Patsy Frasier deals primarily with the Boeing people. She's on vacation this week. The other four take care of the smaller contracts."

"I see. I've met Mr. Flint. He seems very capable." Cynthia chuckled deep in her throat. It was a sound that sent a shiver down Kaitlan's spine. For a second she wondered what Cynthia sounded like in bed, then shook the thought away and concentrated her gaze through the glass office front to a painting hanging on the lobby wall.

"He is very capable. Spent twenty years in the Air Force, then came to us. A good man. All of my

11

people are good. I won't have any other kind. I expect competence, efficiency and thoroughness."

Her gaze pierced the fog that persisted around Kaitlan's thoughts. Their eyes met and locked. For a long instant Kaitlan couldn't move, couldn't speak, couldn't breathe. Then Cynthia's eyes flicked away and she pursed her lips.

"These files that Meg brought me, are these clients I'm to deal with directly?" Kaitlan forced herself to focus on her job, not an easy task when her long celibate libido was in the presence of such a drop-dead beautiful woman, even if that woman was her supervisor.

"Yes. I've had Meg give you a light schedule this week, to give you a chance to settle in and get accustomed to the office." She paused again, a long silent pause during which Kaitlan felt the tension develop in the air. "I'll be perfectly honest with you, Kaitlan. We usually promote from within; I'd rather have put one of my people into your position. I don't know what the folks upstairs were thinking when they hired you, but I have to live with that decision. Don't make me regret that any more than I already do."

Kaitlan flushed, this time with anger. "I am perfectly capable of doing this job, Ms. Perry. You won't regret anything."

Cynthia's look was critical, her jaw set strongly. Then she folded her hands in her lap and looked at them. "You have spunk. I'm glad to see that." She looked back up. "You'll need it around here. I trust you've made living arrangements?"

"I've taken a condo on Capitol Hill."

Cynthia raised her eyebrows, and for a split second Kaitlan thought she had blown it. Seattle's Capitol Hill was the heart of the gay district, and anyone who had lived in Seattle for more than a few months knew it. "A bit of a commute, isn't it?"

"A bit. I don't mind traffic. It gives me a chance to think."

"I see. Well, why don't you peruse those files, and I'll send Meg in to get you when I've arranged that tour." She stood, and Kaitlan stood also. "Again, welcome aboard. I hope we can work well together."

"I'm sure we can, Cynthia," Kaitlan responded smoothly, although her heart was pounding and she felt weak in the knees at the thought of the sort of work they could do well together. It was a strange mixed sensation, her desire and the lingering anger at Cynthia's tone and attitude earlier.

They shook hands, and Kaitlan watched Cynthia's hips carry her out of the office before she sank down into her chair and analyzed her new supervisor.

Cool, competent, not afraid to speak her mind. Attributes that had probably earned her a reputation for being a bitch. Kaitlan felt they could work together, providing Cynthia proved to be fair and even handed as well.

She obviously recognized her own weaknesses, her size and sex being two major ones, and had overcome them. Her handshake had indicated that while she could be strong, she was willing to be cooperative, her

13

body language appeared practiced to give the best impression at all times.

Kaitlan wondered idly what she was like after office hours, when she didn't have to compensate for her gender just to do a job that had nothing to do with gender.

She wondered what Cynthia looked like in a pair of jeans and a blouse, and was struck with a sudden vision of wrapping her arms around her tiny waist and pressing her lips to Cynthia's soft mouth. She put her head in her hands. She had to get herself under control, and fast.

Kaitlan had one big policy where dating was concerned; never, never, never get involved with someone you work with.

Especially not when that someone is the Vice President of Accounts, your direct supervisor.

And especially, especially not when the Vice President of Accounts wears an expensive-looking diamond and a delicately engraved gold wedding band on her left ring finger.

II.

"Good morning, Meg." Kaitlan raised her hand in greeting as she passed the receptionist's desk. Meg returned the salute with a stack of messages and mail.

"You have a ten o'clock and an eleven fifteen, Ms. Davis. And Mr. Flint wanted you to look over a contract with him."

"Happy Friday to you, too," Kaitlan grumbled, though smilingly. "Bring me a latte when you get a second, would you?"

"Of course."

Kaitlan went back to her office, waving at William, who was on the phone, and Robert Mackay, another of the reps. She dropped the pile of mail and messages on her desk, pulled off her coat, and sat down to sort through her calls.

She had met everyone in the office over the past week except for Patsy Frasier, who was due back from vacation today. The other five representatives were all men, but working for Cynthia seemed to have muted any outright hostility they had for a female supervisor.

Kaitlan was glad she hadn't had to break any ground in that department. It was bad enough that she felt like an outsider. There was a great deal of camaraderie among the reps, and Kaitlan felt she wasn't accepted quite as well as she could have been because she came from elsewhere.

She had avoided Cynthia as much as possible, which wasn't too difficult, as Cynthia seemed to constantly be in one meeting or another. But every time she saw her boss, her heart started thudding again and she felt her hands shaking.

It was ridiculous, she thought, to be acting this way over a straight woman. She'd been in town long enough to feel settled, she ought to start going out. Friends had invited her to Wildrose twice, and both times she had begged off. The next time she'd better say yes.

Meg arrived with her latte, with William Flint trailing behind. Kaitlan indicated a chair and he sat. She came around and took the other seat, so that the desk wouldn't be between them.

"Meg said you wanted me to look over a contract?"

"Yes," William replied. "I thought you might like to take a look at how we handle the military end of things. It's a confusing morass of paperwork and red tape, but that's why I'm here." He handed over a thick sheaf of papers.

"Yowza. I hope this isn't a contract for hammers."

William smiled. "No. It's a contract for a replacement part on the ECS used by the Air Force's

KC-135Q tankers. The part's about three inches long."

"Oh." She scanned the paperwork, noting that most of it had military DD form numbers on it. She asked a few questions on the technical aspects of the contract, which William answered thoroughly, then leaned back and put the contract in her lap and reached for her latte. "I don't envy you, William."

"Nobody does. I wish I could say the same for you."

Something in his normally pleasant tone made Kaitlan straighten up. "What do you mean?"

"You haven't met Patsy Frasier yet. She was Cynthia's recommendation for this position. She'd been politicking for it from the moment we found out Bob - your predecessor - was leaving. She isn't too happy that they brought someone in from the outside."

"Cynthia? Or Patsy?" Kaitlan forced herself to act as though this news didn't bother her.

"Both. But I was referring to Patsy. I'd watch my back, if I were you, for a while. Until she gets it out of her system."

"Thanks for the warning, William. I'm sure we can come to an understanding. After all, I didn't purposely take the job away from her."

William just nodded and stood up. "I'm sure you will. From what I've seen so far, you're a good supervisor. Patsy won't be able to help but like you."

"Thanks for the compliment. May I keep this to peruse?" Kaitlan held up the contract and William nodded.

"I need it back by five, though."

"Of course."

William left and Kaitlan went back around her desk and sank down into her chair, turned and looked out the window. She liked the view from her office; she had discovered that the field contained cattle, and watching them meander around was relaxing.

She hadn't been alone more than five minutes when someone rapped at the door. Kaitlan turned back and saw a woman standing there expectantly.

"I'm Patsy Frasier." She was short, thick, with graying brown hair and round glasses over blinking brown eyes. Her suit was impeccably tailored, but it left the impression in Kaitlan's mind of a girl dressing up in her mother's clothes. It didn't fit with her body.

"Come in." Kaitlan rose to shake hands. Patsy transferred her coffee mug to her other hand before taking Kaitlan's outstretched fingers. That's all she shook, just the fingers. But her grip was so tight that Kaitlan bit her lip against the grunt of pain that started to spring out.

"I've been anxious to meet you," Patsy said, settling into one of the chairs. Kaitlan sank back down behind her desk and nodded.

"Likewise. I've heard a lot about you."

Patsy laughed, a not all-together displeasing laugh. It put Kaitlan more at ease. "I hope it wasn't all bad."

"Not at all. Your sales figures are very impressive."

"Thank you." The two women studied one another for a moment, and Kaitlan realized with a start that Patsy was assessing her strengths and weaknesses.

She felt like she was in the ring with a professional wrestler, and one false move would result in a painful body slam to the mat. Kaitlan bent her head for a second and shuffled a few files around on her desk to while she regained her composure.

"Patsy, I understand you wanted this position." She might as well get it out in the open and deal with it before it became a problem. Patsy looked a little taken aback.

"Who told you that?" She removed her glasses and set them on the desk next to the coffee mug she had put there earlier.

"I want you to know that I can sympathize with how you must feel about my having been hired; but it doesn't change the fact that I was hired to do a job. And I intend to do that job to the best of my ability."

Patsy's face hardened. "I'm sure you do."

"I would hope that you will talk with me about any problems you have, so that we can resolve them and can maintain a good working relationship." Kaitlan stood and walked around the desk so that she could sit next to Patsy, hoping to give the impression of equality.

"I was disappointed not to get this promotion," Patsy said carefully. "But there will be other opportunities."

"You're free to talk to me at any time if you want to."

"Thank you. But I'm fine with the arrangements that have been made."

"Good. I'm glad there isn't a problem." She smiled.

Patsy smiled back and reached for her glasses. Her hand hit the coffee mug, knocking it over and sending coffee spilling across Kaitlan's desk. "Oh, no!"

"Damn." Kaitlan leapt toward the contract William had left. Patsy was diving for the desk as well. The two women collided, and Kaitlan almost ended up on the floor. Patsy picked up a folder that was covered with coffee. As she did so, it ran off the edges, splashing over more files. "Patsy - leave it."

"I'm so sorry, Kaitlan. I'm half blind without my glasses."

Kaitlan set her jaw and forced herself to stay calm. "It's all right, Patsy. Really. I'll take care of it."

"I am sorry...." Kaitlan waved her away as she picked up William's now coffee-stained contract and looked at it ruefully. Patsy withdrew, still muttering, and Kaitlan stood staring at her desk. Everything on it lay in a puddle of brown liquid.

With a silent curse, Kaitlan turned on her heel and strode out of the office. She went to the restroom and grabbed a fistful of paper towels, then returned to her desk and tried to mop up the spill.

After the coffee was gone, she stared down at the remaining mess. Not only was everything splattered with brown spots, the coffee had been extremely sweet, and everything was sticky. Kaitlan piled together the folders and headed toward Meg's desk.

"What happened?" Meg's face was inquisitive as she looked at the stack of files.

"Patsy Frasier 'accidentally' spilled her coffee," Kaitlan said, growling. "Some of these aren't even legible any more. And my keyboard needs cleaned."

"I can get replacements - but it's going to take a while."

"Kaitlan." Cynthia's voice came calmly from her doorway. "Would you step into my office for a moment?"

When the door had closed behind them, Kaitlan let out a long angry sigh. "She ruined Flint's contract."

Cynthia crossed to her desk and sat down on the edge of it. The slit in her skirt opened to reveal an expanse of firm thigh, but Kaitlan was too angry to take more than a cursory notice. "Patsy is something of a klutz. I wouldn't be too angry. The files can be replaced."

"She had just finished telling me she didn't have a problem with me, and then this happens. What am I supposed to think? Why didn't you tell me someone from this office had been recommended for the position?" Cynthia pursed her lips.

"It didn't seem necessary. Of course I recommended someone. I told you we usually promote from within. Patsy has worked here for fifteen years. She's a very capable salesperson, and I thought she would make a capable supervisor." She crossed her arms, and Kaitlan couldn't help but notice the defensiveness of the posture.

"Capable or not, she spilled an entire cup of coffee on my desk."

"Did she apologize?"

"Of course she did." Kaitlan began to feel like she was over reacting. Cynthia, despite her body

21

language, seemed unaffected by the incident. "I just want to know one thing."

"That is?"

"Is Patsy your protégé? Am I to be expected to let her slide where I wouldn't let the others? Tell me now, before something else happens."

Cynthia stood up and crossed to the large window behind her desk. She stared out across the parking lot for a long silent moment. When she turned back around, her face was red. Her voice shook with barely contained anger. "I do not have 'pets' in this office, Ms. Davis. Patsy pulls her weight the same as everyone else. I did not become a vice president by playing favorites, I got where I am by treating everyone the same. I expect you to do so as well. I'd better not hear about you singling anyone, and I mean anyone out for special treatment, good or bad. Is that clear, Ms. Davis?"

Kaitlan, her face as red as Cynthia's, nodded stiffly. "Perfectly clear, Ms. Perry."

"That will be all."

Kaitlan turned and marched out of the office, fuming silently. Meg glanced at her then dropped her head and pretended to be busy. Kaitlan crossed to her office and closed the door roughly behind her, then collapsed into her chair and spun to face out the window.

Special treatment, indeed. It was clear to her who got special treatment. *Poor Patsy, so clumsy.* Never mind that she shouldn't have brought a full cup of coffee into someone else's office. Never mind that she had no reason to take off her glasses if she was half blind without them.

Kaitlan caught herself as she started to rub her hands across her face, knowing it would ruin her makeup. Instead, she rubbed the arms of the chair and tried to relax. She had no doubts that Patsy would run right past her to Cynthia if she didn't like something Kaitlan was doing, and she had no doubts who Cynthia would back up.

"Damn office politics," Kaitlan muttered, staring out the window. Part of her anger stemmed from disappointment in Cynthia, who had seemed so perfect up to that point. To find out that Cynthia had favorites, just like every other boss, was a let down.

Though why trim, beautiful Cynthia would pick dowdy, nervous Patsy was beyond Kaitlan. Unless it was because Patsy was the only other woman in the office; or had been until Kaitlan arrived.

The thought briefly ran across Kaitlan's mind that the pair could be lovers, but the thought kept running. Cynthia was straight. Kaitlan had seen a photograph of her and a handsome man standing together, hanging on her office wall, and another picture of two smiling teenagers on her desk.

Kaitlan sighed and stretched, then turned back to her desk and finished cleaning it up. She had a ten o'clock appointment with a client and she wanted to scan the technical literature before presenting it to him.

She was halfway through the tech data when Cynthia walked into her office. She didn't knock; she just walked in and sat herself down in one of the chairs.

"What do you need, Ms. Perry?" Kaitlan dropped her gaze to her paperwork again, deliberately ignoring the other woman. Cynthia was quiet for a moment, and very still.

"Put that down."

"I have an appointment to prepare for."

"Kaitlan, put it down." Kaitlan glanced up and caught part of a look Cynthia was giving her, a look that sent a shiver of hunger through her body. She put down the tech manual and folded her hands in front of her on the desk.

"What do you need?" she repeated.

"I want to apologize for my outburst earlier. It wasn't called for. In my position, I have to be very careful about accusations of favoritism."

"I'm sure you do," Kaitlan said, somewhat harshly. Cynthia reddened.

"You've only been here a week, Kaitlan. Don't you think you ought to wait until you know how things operate a little bit better before you start hurling accusations?"

"I suppose I should," Kaitlan admitted. "But I have a feeling Patsy Frasier is going to be running over my head every time she disagrees with me. That doesn't make me very comfortable."

"I believe in the chain of command in this office, Kaitlan. I honestly don't play favorites. And I don't want to alienate you. I like you."

Whoa, Kaitlan thought, *what's this all about?* "What

does that mean? Have I passed some sort of test?"

"No. It simply means that I like you. It so happens that I like you a lot. I sense - we may be kindred spirits." Kaitlan caught the same look in her eyes, and felt a swirling confusion that intensified as her gaze dropped again to the diamond ring and wedding band on Cynthia's finger.

What is Cynthia playing at? Was this an attempt to see how Kaitlan would react to being flirted with, had Cynthia found out Kaitlan was gay? "I'm glad, Cynthia. It helps our working relationship if we like each other, don't you think?"

Cynthia frowned slightly. "Yes. Of course it does. But I was thinking more on a personal level. I was going to ask if you played tennis."

Kaitlan thought furiously, trying to distinguish between what Cynthia was saying and what she herself was reading into it. "I - ah - yes, I play tennis."

"Good. Then perhaps we can get together for a match."

"I don't - that is - I try to keep my personal life separate from my work," Kaitlan said weakly, wanting very much to leap at the opportunity to spend time with the woman opposite her.

"And you never make exceptions?" Kaitlan shook her head. "Too bad." Cynthia glanced at her watch and stood. "I'd better let you finish reading that wonderfully entertaining tech manual."

"Yes." Kaitlan couldn't say anything else. She watched Cynthia cross to the door, then set her face abruptly when she turned back.

"I still like you." With that, she was gone. Kaitlan let her breath out slowly and calmed herself, then picked up the manual she was reading and forced herself to sink back into it.

III.

"... and then she up and asked me to play tennis." Kaitlan was pacing back and forth across the bedroom floor talking into her cordless phone while undressing. "Honestly, Lynda, I didn't know what to do."

"Say yes, for crying out loud," her friend replied.

"She's my boss. I don't get involved with people I work with."

"She didn't ask you to sleep with her, Kaitlan. Playing tennis would be considered good form among most circles. Especially with the boss." Kaitlan sighed and stepped out of her skirt, then bent to pull off her pantyhose. She reached for her slacks.

"I just didn't expect it. Maybe it wasn't the most politically correct thing to do. I was going from my gut."

"No you weren't," Lynda replied sartorially. "From what I've heard, your gut would have said 'yes, please and take me home afterwards.'"

"Actually, I was so mad I wanted to tell her to go to hell." Kaitlan held the phone between her shoulder and ear as she sat down on the bed to slip on her shoes. "She did an amazing turn around on me."

"Are you so sure she's straight?"

"I saw the ring. And the picture with the husband. Yeah, she's straight. I almost think she was toying with me, seeing how I'd react."

"You're paranoid. Play tennis with the woman, Kaitlan. Not everyone is out to screw you, literally or figuratively."

"Easy for you to say." Kaitlan thought of Dana, and immediately wished she hadn't. Lynda was silent on the other end of the line. "Okay, maybe you're right. I guess I just need to start making the social rounds, get back into the scene here. Start dating."

"Aha! You've gotten past the block with the 'D' word. Good. Alex and I are going on a harbor cruise next week. I can still get you a ticket if you want. It includes dinner and dancing. Lesbians only. Maybe you'll meet Ms. Right. Or at least Ms. Right Now."

"Okay. Count me in." She frowned at her reflection in the mirror. "But if I meet Ms. Right, I'll give you fifty dollars."

"Oh, ye of little faith."

"Me of no faith," Kaitlan responded. "My faith is living in Arizona with Dana Louise Mitchum and Officer Rebecca Colwell." She was surprised at the bitterness still in her voice, even after so long.

"Oh, Kaitlan...." Lynda sounded exasperated.

"Yeah, old wounds. I know."

"So promise me you'll play tennis with this Cynthia Perry woman."

"I promise." Kaitlan said good-bye after promising

again, and changed her shirt, then wandered toward the kitchen looking for some dinner.

She had taken a lease on a two bedroom one level condo, and as she wound her way through the living room, she couldn't help but think how different it was from the old four-bedroom Victorian she and Dana had owned in Spokane.

What precious little furniture was left was sitting haphazardly around the living room, most of it hidden under piles of boxes that had yet to be unpacked. Kaitlan stopped in the middle of the room, looked around, and remembered.

She remembered how she and Dana had lovingly restored the old house one room at a time, remembered the take-out pizzas they had eaten amidst piles of plaster and dust, the bottles of wine shared to christen each room as the last coat of paint dried, the joy in choosing furnishings, many of them antiques.

The house had been warm and comfortable, just like their relationship. In twelve years, Kaitlan had never even owned a pair of pajamas. They had always kept each other warm through the cold Spokane winters. The house was hostess to dinner parties and planning groups, birthdays and funeral gatherings, wedding dinners and baby showers.

It had been snowing fiercely that afternoon, Kaitlan remembered. She was glad to finally pull into the driveway, anxious to warm herself with a cup of hot tea and a long cuddle with Dana. She walked into the kitchen through the back door, and promptly dropped her briefcase.

Her first thought was that there had been a robbery, that Dana might be injured. She had mentioned taking the day off to do some housework. As she raced through the house, through room after room almost totally devoid of furniture, of anything, her heart was in her throat, fearing what she would find around the next turn.

It wasn't until she stood in the master bedroom, staring at the untidy pile of clothing in the middle of the room, all of it belonging to her, that the significance of everything began to sink in. She turned and went slowly back down the stairs and to the kitchen. There, on the counter, was a thick envelope. With trembling hands, Kaitlan opened it.

Dear Kaitlan:

By the time you read this we'll be gone. I'm sorry that things have to work out this way, but I just couldn't find the words to tell you before, and I think this is for the best. You'll find enclosed papers I had drawn up for the sale of the house. Notice I've signed them already, and that you'll get 70 percent of the proceeds. I hope that will make up for the furniture.

Please understand that this is something I had to do. I never meant for it to happen, but it did. I'm not going to tell you who she is, just know that she loves me and I love her. But I still love you. I always will. That's why I have to leave. I have to leave while it's still good between us, before it turns sour like I know it has to eventually.

Dana

Kaitlan had stared at the letter for a long time before crying. It hadn't taken her long to find out who 'she' was; everyone she knew admitted knowledge of the affair between Dana and Rebecca. Numb with shock, she sold the house and moved into an apartment.

And now into a condo; a small step up. Kaitlan wrapped her arms around herself and surveyed the room. It would do for now, until she decided where she wanted to buy. Impatiently, she shook herself and turned toward the kitchen.

There was nothing appetizing in the freezer, and the refrigerator was empty save for a bottle of wine. She loved to cook, but cooking for one just didn't hold the same allure, and she had been postponing doing her grocery shopping. With a disgusted sigh, Kaitlan grabbed a sweatshirt. Maybe one of the restaurants on Broadway would tempt her palate.

IV.

All during the Monday morning staff meeting Kaitlan fidgeted and tried not to lose her nerve. Every time Cynthia turned to look at her, Kaitlan could see the strange expression that crossed her face, something akin to disappointment.

Patsy sat looking fierce at the far end of the large conference table, her arms crossed over her gray business suit. Kaitlan was again struck with an image of dishevelment, even though Patsy's dress was immaculate. She kept her gaze directly ahead, never looking at Kaitlan.

After the meeting was over, Kaitlan swallowed her reserve and followed Cynthia to her office. At the door, Cynthia turned and looked her up and down. "Are you sick?"

"No." Kaitlan was startled. "Why?"

"You've had the queerest look on your face all morning. I thought you were going to bolt out of the conference room at any moment."

"Can we - step inside?" She indicated Cynthia's office. Cynthia pushed open the door and stepped aside to allow Kaitlan past.

As she brushed by the darker woman, her nose was filled with the same scent as she had noticed on Cynthia before. It almost smelled like Patchouli, but not quite. Abruptly, she felt unsure about what she was there for. Her eyes sought out the photograph on the wall and she forced herself into a silent litany. *She's straight.*

Cynthia closed the door and went to the long sideboard that ran along one wall. On it was a silver coffee service. "Would you like a cup of coffee?"

"Yes, please." She watched Cynthia gracefully pour two cups of coffee, then accepted the cup her supervisor handed her. She declined cream or sugar, and blew gently across the top of the coffee to cool it.

"What's troubling you?"

"Nothing. I spent the weekend thinking about your invitation. I should apologize. I'd like to play tennis with you some afternoon."

Kaitlan watched Cynthia's expression slowly change, watched the smile spread across her face. It was the first real smile she had seen on the woman, and the even whiteness of her teeth lit her features until she almost glowed. "I'm glad you changed your mind."

"I was upset Friday about Patsy. I shouldn't have been. I took that out on you and I'm sorry."

"It's quite all right. Friends, then?"

"Friends." Kaitlan took a sip of her coffee and

hoped she wasn't making a big mistake.

*   *   *   *   *

"Deuce," Kaitlan called when the ball Cynthia had hit landed inches over the service line. She went to retrieve it and trotted back to the line. "Yet again."

"That makes what, the sixth time? Hurry up and lose." Cynthia wiped her forehead with her sleeve and set herself to receive the serve.

"Why don't you lose?" Before Cynthia could answer, Kaitlan bent to the ready. She let loose with a grunt as she powered the ball over the net. Cynthia's arm muscles flexed as she hit a two-handed return.

Kaitlan hit a lob and waited for Cynthia to chase it down. Her eyes followed the movement of her opponent's chest as she stretched to hit the ball, and almost missed her own return.

A moment later, Cynthia put one into the net. "Damn!"

"Add in," Kaitlan called, grinning. "Surrender now?"

"Never," Cynthia returned, walking toward the net. She tossed the ball back to Kaitlan and winked. "I never give up."

Kaitlan didn't catch the ball. It bounced past her as she stood rooted to the spot, watching the smooth side-to-side movement of Cynthia's hips, her mind replaying the wink.

She was a better tennis player than Cynthia. She knew this because she hadn't been able to concentrate on the game at all, and they were tied neck and neck in the last game of the match.

She'd lost her concentration the moment Cynthia had taken off her running suit to reveal her shorts and sports top. And all through the match, she'd been distracted by Cynthia's movements. The sweat that beaded Kaitlan's brow didn't come entirely from exertion.

"Kaitlan? Hello, anybody home?"

Kaitlan shook herself and turned to get the balls. They were playing indoors at Cynthia's sports club, which was good as far as Kaitlan was concerned because it was raining and about thirty-six degrees outside.

She decided she'd better hurry up and win the game, because their court time was almost up. She stepped to the line, studied where her opponent was standing ready, and hit a spinning serve that landing just inside the line and continued on past a startled looking Cynthia.

"Game, set and match," Kaitlan called, feeling only a little bit underhanded for the ace.

"Where did that come from? You've been holding out on me." Cynthia came to the net and they shook hands. Kaitlan grinned.

"Only a little. It isn't polite to beat the boss too badly."

For just a moment, Cynthia appeared to consider how truthful she was being, and then she smiled too. "Okay, Martina."

Kaitlan coughed to hide the flush that started up

her cheeks. "Hardly. She's better looking than I am."

"You're pretty good looking when you blush, Kaitlan. It makes your eyes bluer." Kaitlan went completely red. Cynthia studied her for a scant second, then tossed her head and laughed. "I didn't mean to embarrass you."

"You didn't," Kaitlan mumbled.

"I packed a picnic lunch, but it doesn't appear we can eat it outside." They could both hear the steady drum of rain on the metal roof of the building. "So why don't we go to your condo? It's closest."

"I - ah - that is...."

Cynthia raised both eyebrows. "Bad idea? Don't want me to meet your boyfriend?"

"No, nothing like that. I'm still living out of boxes, to be honest. And I don't have a boyfriend." Kaitlan was willing to admit that much. Cynthia considered for a minute.

"Oh, well. It was just a thought. Good game, by the way."

They walked back to the locker room. Inside, they went to their respective lockers and gathered their gear. In the lobby, staring out at the pouring rain, Kaitlan almost gave in. But she had to draw the line somewhere, and her condo was a good place.

"I'll see you tomorrow, Cynthia."

"Yes. Bright and early. Oh, by the way Kaitlan...." Kaitlan turned and saw Cynthia's eyes moving slowly up her body. They reached her face and Cynthia smiled again. "You're pretty good looking whether you're blushing or not. Better looking than Martina, if you ask me."

Before Kaitlan could frame an appropriate response, a taller woman in a jogging suit who descended upon them from the area of the weight machines accosted the pair.

"Cynthia! Why, it's been months. How are you?"

"I'm fine, Margo. How's John?" Cynthia looked faintly uneasy.

"He's just fine. We've been meaning to invite you and Paul over for dinner."

Cynthia's face flared into redness. Kaitlan stared at her for just a moment then, cursing herself for misunderstanding Cynthia's message, turned toward the door.

"I have to go, Cynthia," she mumbled. Shouldering her gear bag, she pushed out the door and into the rain before Cynthia could respond.

V.

Kaitlan met Lynda and Alex at the pier. The motor cruiser that was to host the dinner and dance bobbed gently up and down, bumping occasionally against it's mooring with a squeaking of plastic. Deep within her own thoughts, Kaitlan jumped when Lynda touched her arm.

"Hi. Nervous?"

"A little," Kaitlan admitted. "It's been a long time since I was out like this." She glanced around and stuck her hands into her coat pockets. "I didn't have much chance to wear my tails in Spokane. Dana - didn't like me to."

"You look fine." Lynda leaned over and adjusted the red bow tie Kaitlan wore with her black formal. Lynda herself wore tails, while Alex had opted for an evening dress. Around them milled other couples in formal wear. There was a short blast from the ship's horn. "Come on, they're leaving."

Kaitlan said hello to Alex as the trio walked toward the gangplank. Once on board, Kaitlan made her way directly to the bar and ordered a glass of wine. She turned and saw Lynda coming up behind her. Her friend ordered two drinks, then leaned against the bar and looked at her. Below their feet, the deck vibrated as the twin diesel engines hummed into life and the ship began to ease away from the dock.

"It looks to me that I'm the only single person here," Kaitlan commented. Lynda surveyed the crowd and shrugged.

"Possibly. But I doubt it. Pat said they sold sixty tickets. A good turnout, don't you think?"

At two hundred fifty dollars each, that was a very good turnout. "Yes. What's the LRC using the funds for again?" The Lesbian Resource Center, where Alex worked as a lawyer, was sponsoring the event as a fundraiser, but Kaitlan had no idea what specifically her dollars were going toward.

"The battered women's shelter." Lynda adjusted her tie. "About time someone funded it. Come on, I'll start introducing you around."

The dinner bell rang at seven, and Kaitlan followed her friends to their assigned table. There were ten in the dining room, each seating six people. Theirs was against the window, where they could look out over the lights of the city.

As they approached, wending their way through the maze of people, Kaitlan saw that three of the seats were already taken. Two of the women wore dresses and the third was in a white tuxedo. They drew closer, and Kaitlan began to get a strange feeling in her stomach. The woman sitting closest to her, with her back to them, seemed familiar. The woman in white saw them and stood up.

"Ah, our dinner companions. Hi Alex."

"Hello, Jenny, Trish." Alex went around to hug her friend and Kaitlan put her hand on the closest vacant seat to allow Lynda to sit next to Jenny. This put her next to the familiar woman, who turned as she started to sit down. Abruptly, Kaitlan felt lightheaded. She sank into her chair, unable to speak.

"Kaitlan? Are you all right?" Lynda sounded concerned. Kaitlan, unable to tear her eyes from Cynthia's, tried to swallow and nodded her head. Cynthia was turning bright red.

"Hello, Kaitlan," she managed weakly. Kaitlan nodded again. "What a surprise."

"Yes." Not allowing the rush of images that flooded her mind to overwhelm her, Kaitlan remembered Paul. "Quite a surprise."

"You two know each other?" Jenny said, and laughed.

"We're - business acquaintances, yes," Kaitlan replied. She forced herself to look away. Lynda's eyes showed that she knew exactly who Cynthia was, but she tactfully kept her mouth closed.

"Well, Cyn, you said you wouldn't know anyone. Aren't you glad we made you come with us?" Jenny said, still smiling. Kaitlan wondered if she suspected some sort of involvement between Cynthia and herself.

"Oh, overjoyed." Cynthia's voice was sarcastic.

The salads were already on the tables, and Kaitlan picked up her fork and started poking at hers. Cynthia followed suit, and the remaining four, sensing the tension, began to talk among themselves about the LRC.

Kaitlan's mind whirled. Cynthia was the absolute last person she would have expected to see on a lesbian dinner cruise. Yet here she was sitting next to her. Kaitlan felt awkward, not knowing what to say or do. Her body was sending out strong signals of desire, worse than even the first day they had met.

But her mind was flashing warning signs. She began to dissect everything she could remember Cynthia ever saying to her, looking for clues, hints, anything. There had been none. True, Cynthia had told her she was good looking, but that hardly counted.

The main course was delivered, and Kaitlan automatically cut into her prime rib, eating distractedly, not tasting her food at all. She wondered how she should handle the situation. Not one to shrink from trouble, she began to plan how she should approach Cynthia about Paul. Was Cynthia even gay?

Conversation swirled around and Kaitlan participated as best she could, but couldn't turn her thoughts from Cynthia, who remained silent except when directly spoken to.

Cynthia was wearing an evening gown, a black off the shoulder dress of modest design that showed of her cleavage to wonderful advantage. But it didn't look like the dress a femme would wear. It looked like a dress a wife would wear.

She could just be along for the ride with friends. Or she could be bisexual. Kaitlan shivered. She didn't want to think about Cynthia as being bi-. She was trying not to think about Cynthia at all.

"I think I need some air," Cynthia's voice interrupted her thoughts and she realized she had finished her dinner without even noticing. "Would you mind escorting me, Kaitlan?"

Focusing finally on Cynthia's face, Kaitlan nodded and stood up, offering her hand. Cynthia took it, and Kaitlan felt a warm ball begin to tumble in her stomach. They had shaken hands, but the feeling of just holding her hand to help her up was different entirely.

Standing, Cynthia slipped her arm through Kaitlan's and indicated the door to the outside deck. They walked through it in silence, then Kaitlan turned her loose and Cynthia crossed to the railing and leaned against it momentarily.

"I had no idea you were a lesbian," she said. "This is a shock."

"You're telling me." Kaitlan paused, then asked bluntly, "Why are you here?" Cynthia turned back to her. "I would think you'd have better things to do than to associate with a bunch of lesbians."

"What are you talking about - oh, Paul. I never explained Paul."

Kaitlan nodded. "Yes, Paul."

Cynthia drew in a deep breath. "We're in the middle of a divorce."

"Then why do you have that picture in the office? Why do you wear those rings?" Kaitlan knew she didn't have any right to be asking those kinds of questions, but something in her had to know and

Cynthia seemed willing to answer.

"I'm not out at work, Kaitlan, and I recommend that you not come out either. I will always have that picture of Paul in my office. He's my insurance policy."

Kaitlan frowned. "What do you mean, don't come out at work? Why not?"

"If you want to get promoted, don't come out. If you do come out ... Kaitlan, please. I've spent too many years getting where I am. Don't bring me out with you."

Kaitlan studied her for a long moment. "Why the hell would I do that?"

"I don't know. But I know people it's happened to."

They were silent for a while. It was chilly, and Cynthia started to shiver. "Maybe we should go back in," Kaitlan suggested. Cynthia shook her head.

"I was very uncomfortable coming to this. I'd rather stay out here and recoup my energy for a while. Jenny assures me my dance card will be filled and I need to be prepared."

"I'm sure it will be." Cynthia was still shivering and Kaitlan instinctively removed her jacket and slipped it around the slighter woman's shoulders. Cynthia wrapped it around her with a grateful smile.

"Quite the gentleman, aren't you," she commented. Kaitlan blushed.

"I guess I'm old fashioned. I hate to see a lady standing in the cold."

"At least I'm not alone." Cynthia looked up at her. "Thank you for coming with me."

"My pleasure." Kaitlan meant it. She took a step closer and leaned against the railing. Cynthia moved next to her and they stood, shoulder to shoulder, staring out at the lights over the sound.

"I meant it when I said I liked you," Cynthia said a little later, "I should have ... I mean .... Oh, damn."

Kaitlan glanced over to find her companion quite red. "What's wrong?"

Cynthia was slow to answer. "I've only been out for a year or so," she finally responded. "I'm not well attuned to my signals. When I said I liked you, I meant it socially. That's all. Now ... now that I've found out...."

"Now that you've found out, what?" Kaitlan felt a little uneasy.

"There's more to it now."

"My partner left me ten months ago," Kaitlan chose her words carefully. "We had been together for twelve years. Since then, I haven't really had much interest in anyone."

"That might explain the increase in your sales figures," Cynthia said, and smiled.

"It might." Kaitlan smiled back, ruefully.

"Well, I still think you're a damn good supervisor."

"Thank you."

Another pause. "Would you like to go for coffee after we dock?"

Kaitlan struggled with herself, part of her wanting badly to say yes, part of her knowing she shouldn't. "I'm afraid I can't. I'm sorry, Cynthia, I really can't. It isn't that I don't want to...."

"I shouldn't have asked."

"That isn't it." The breeze shifted direction and Kaitlan was again aware of the scent Cynthia wore as it drifted past her nose. It brought up a flash of desire so brilliant and sudden that Kaitlan took a physical step from the power of it.

Unfortunately, the step she took put her even closer to the source. Almost in Cynthia's arms, Kaitlan looked down at her and swallowed against the ache she felt.

"Kaitlan...." Cynthia's eyes were wide, but she made no attempt to move away. Kaitlan put her hands on Cynthia's shoulders and stared into her face.

"It would be so easy to fall into your eyes and drown," she said. "And I don't think I would fight at all."

"Kaitlan." Her name was a caress. Cynthia reached up to cover her hands. They stared at each other for a long moment.

"Oh, God," Kaitlan whispered finally, and bent her head. Cynthia met her kiss halfway, and for a moment, nothing existed but the warmth of their lips pressed together. Then a cold breeze whipped past them, bringing a blast of reality into Kaitlan's mind. She stepped away and turned, putting distance between herself and Cynthia.

"What is it?"

"I can't - I can't do this," Kaitlan stammered. "I shouldn't have kissed you, I'm sorry."

"I'm not." It sounded as though Cynthia was having trouble speaking, but Kaitlan didn't want to look. She dropped her head and stared at the deck. "Kaitlan, there's nothing to be sorry for."

"Yes, there is." Kaitlan looked at her. "I don't get involved with co-workers. You're my boss, Cynthia. That's playing with dynamite."

Cynthia frowned. "So that's it, is it? Well, I can't blame you for that." She took off Kaitlan's coat and handed it back to her. "The dancing has started. I think we'd better go in."

"Cynthia...." Cynthia glanced at her. "In any other circumstances.... You're a very attractive woman."

"Thank you, Kaitlan. I'll see you Monday morning." She walked away. Kaitlan pulled on her jacket and started after her, then stamped her foot and spun back toward the rail, angry with herself. For a long while she stared out over the water, half-listening to the music from inside the large main cabin.

"Well, here you are." Alex's voice was quiet. She stepped up next to Kaitlan and looked out at the skyline of Seattle. "Lynda was getting worried you might have thrown yourself overboard."

Kaitlan laughed, sarcastically. "Well, I went overboard, that's for sure."

"Hmm-hmm. Care to discuss that comment?"

"Alex, you're a dear friend...." She looked away.

"But?" Alex's gaze joined hers on the bright lights of a ferry as it passed in the distance.

"But I don't think I want to talk about it."

Alex nodded sagely and was silent. A moment later she said, "She's a very good looking woman, isn't she?"

"Yes, she is, damn it all. Christ! Why did she have to be here?" Kaitlan turned her back to the water and stared through the glass into the crowded cabin.

Alex glanced at her. "A past problem or an unresolved one?"

"She's ... a dilemma."

"Ah, one of those. Look, it's freezing out here. Come back in and dance with me. I can't let you get away without at least one dance."

Kaitlan sighed and turned to look at her friend. She forced a grin and nodded. "Okay. You look real femme in that dress, by the way. How'd Lynda get you into it?"

Alex laughed as they started toward the door. "She told me exactly how she was going to get me out of it when we got home tonight."

Kaitlan caught sight of Cynthia as they went back to the table. She was on the dance floor with someone and Kaitlan was surprised to feel a shock of jealousy as the stranger's arm slid around Cynthia's waist to spin her. Cynthia was laughing.

Kaitlan sat abruptly and reached for her wine.

"My, there's an expression for you." Lynda's tone was only half-joking. Kaitlan frowned and ducked her head, irritated with herself for her lack of self-control.

"If we weren't in the middle of the Puget Sound I'd be out of here," she growled. "This was a bad idea."

"Well, relax. We'll be back soon enough."

Kaitlan rubbed her face and hoped so.

47

VI.

Flipping on the light switch, Kaitlan slammed the front door closed and leaned against it, her breath leaving her in an explosive sigh. The evening had seemed interminable. Every sight of Cynthia had brought a fresh thrill of desire.

Pushing off, Kaitlan went to the kitchen and poured a glass of wine. Sipping at it, she stared at the pile of empty boxes in the corner, at the dishes from breakfast that were still undone in the sink, at the basket of clothes on the table. Good that she had things to keep her busy over the weekend. Otherwise she was afraid she might spend the next two days doing nothing but moping and thinking about Dana.

Taking her wine into the bedroom, she stripped and walked naked into the bathroom to turn on the shower. Waiting for the water to warm up, she turned and studied herself in the mirror. As steam started to curl around the room, she found herself remembering the soft pressure of Cynthia's lips beneath hers. To her irritation, her nipples started to harden and sent a rush of warmth toward her groin.

Damn it, Kaitlan cursed herself, *I could have gone*

home with Cynthia instead of spending another night alone. As soon as she thought it she felt ashamed. Kissing Cynthia had been a mistake, and the sooner she accepted that, the better off she'd be.

Stepping into the shower, she felt the hot water sluicing over her body and fought off images of Cynthia's smooth shoulders, the curving shadow of her breasts where they vanished beneath the satin evening gown. How easy it would have been to drop her hands to that slender waist, to pull Cynthia against her, allowing the kiss to go deep and inside...

Stop it! Kaitlan ordered herself. *Stop thinking about it. It's just ten months of celibacy doing this.* She turned her face into the spray and reached for the soap. Cynthia was her supervisor. Period. She could never allow anything to happen between them, should never have given in to the impulse that made her kiss Cynthia in the first place.

As she lathered her body, it became painfully apparent that she was doing no good by trying to deny how that kiss had affected her. Just the touch of the soap on her breast sent a veritable gush of wetness to her groin, a wetness that had nothing to do with the shower. Washing between her legs would be impossible.

Gritting her teeth, Kaitlan turned the hot water completely off and stood shivering under the cold water until the heated desire in her body stilled. Then she stepped out of the shower, toweled off roughly and dressed for bed, finished her wine and turned out the light.

Something woke her early the next morning from a dream in which Cynthia played a prominent role. Groaning, Kaitlan glanced at her alarm clock to find it was only five AM. She rolled onto her back and stared at the ceiling for a moment, wanting to go back to sleep but afraid of resuming the dream that had kindled her desire all over again.

Giving up finally, she got out of bed and padded into the kitchen to make a pot of coffee. If she had to be up at such an ungodly hour on a weekend, she might as well be productive. It would be a good day to organize the place, unpack and so forth. Maybe the physical exertion would help calm her hormones.

It didn't. By six o'clock that evening, Kaitlan had to admit that she was no better off than she would have been if she'd just rolled over and gone back to sleep. The living room was in order; most of her belongings unpacked and put away, and Kaitlan was sitting on the sofa cursing herself yet again for not giving in all the way. And as soon as she finished doing that, she cursed herself for giving in as far as she had.

That night and the next day were no different; but by Sunday night Kaitlan knew she had to get herself under control. She had to do something. As she lay in bed, staring at the wall, she finally surrendered to her need and moved her hand between her legs. She was more than ready as she rolled onto her back, her fingers moving easily.

In the months since Dana's departure, Kaitlan had resorted to self-satisfaction only a couple of times, and this time she felt something close to pain in the

50

desperate need of her body. When at last she reached orgasm, she could not keep the words from her lips, "Cynthia - yes, Cynthia!"

VII.

Kaitlan paced in her office, waiting for time to slide into the Monday morning meeting with a stomach full of butterflies. She dreaded having to face Cynthia after the night before. Even as she lay in the afterglow of orgasm, she had known it had simply dampened her desire, not assuaged it.

But at least she was able to convince herself that the problem was not Cynthia so much as the previous ten months of celibacy. She honestly thought that she would have had the same reaction from kissing Lynda, whom she had never had the slightest desire for. It was the kiss itself, not who was on the other end of it.

Finally, there was no putting off the staff meeting and she went down to the conference room and took her place next to the head chair. When Cynthia came in, she was with Fred, and Kaitlan breathed a quiet sigh of relief that they wouldn't be alone.

"Good morning, Kaitlan," Cynthia said with a wan smile. Kaitlan nodded and started shuffling her papers. Cynthia went to the far side of the table and stood talking with Fred while the others filed in.

The meeting was short and sweet, and Kaitlan looked to escape at the first opportunity, but Cynthia called to her as she started out the door. Slowly, Kaitlan turned around. "Yes, Cynthia?"

"I'd like to see you in my office, please."

"Now?"

"Yes, now." Sighing, Kaitlan went next door to Cynthia's office and waited for her. Cynthia followed her inside and shut the door behind them. "I have a new client for you."

"Oh?" Kaitlan tried to relax, to forget the sensation of Cynthia's mouth on hers that had tormented her all weekend.

"Barbara Small, chief purchasing agent for SouthAlaska Transport. She's flying in from Juneau at one and I want you to meet her and make sure she gets settled in her hotel. I'd give the account to one of the others, but it could work into something big and I wanted to give you first crack at it."

"Thanks. Is there a file?" Cynthia handed her a slim folder. Kaitlan noticed that her hand trembled as she held it out and when Kaitlan took the file, Cynthia pulled back as if she were afraid Kaitlan was going to touch her. "I'll get right on this."

"Good. I know you'll do a great job." She paused. "Kaitlan ... there isn't a problem, is there? You seemed very uncomfortable this morning."

Kaitlan shook her head quickly, not willing to admit that she had been having difficulty concentrating on what was said in the meeting, her attention drawn to Cynthia's face. If she closed her eyes, she was almost certain she could bring an image of that face into sharp focus with ease. Cynthia cocked her head and looked at her for a second.

"All right, then. Knock 'em dead."

"Thanks, Cynthia." Kaitlan fled the office before she could say more. She closed the door to her own office and crossed to the desk, sinking down into her chair and turning to look out the window. The file Cynthia had given her lay unopened on the desk. She sat, unmoving, for a long silent time, fighting the pounding behind her eyes.

*   *   *   *   *

The flight in from Juneau was late, and Kaitlan looked once again at her watch before uncrossing her legs and standing. A couple of other people waiting in the lobby glanced at her curiously as she rubbed her temples and walked over to the window.

Finally, after what seemed like an eternity, the arrival of the commuter plane was announced over the speaker. A few minutes later, a uniformed attendant pushed open the sky gate door and passengers began to file off. Kaitlan scanned the debarkees for someone who looked like a purchasing agent for an air transport company.

A middle-aged woman with a severe bun stepped into the lobby and shifted her briefcase before stepping forward. Kaitlan started to move toward her, certain that she had to be Barbara Small. Before she could speak, however, the woman turned and raised her hand at a tall man in a business suit. Confused, Kaitlan stopped.

"Ms. Davis?" Kaitlan turned and looked at a blue-jeaned woman with blonde hair a few shades lighter than her own who was standing very close to her. She wore a flannel shirt and carried a fleece-lined denim jacket and a briefcase. Behind her round wire-rimmed glasses her green eyes sparked with intelligence.

"Yes," Kaitlan responded, drawing her eyebrows together. The woman stuck out a hand.

"Barb Small, SouthAlaska Transport."

"Kaitlan Davis." They shook. Barbara's grip was firm, but when she let go, she let her fingers trail across the palm of Kaitlan's hand. Kaitlan swallowed and dropped her arm. "I understand you've got a room at the Radisson. I'll give you a ride."

"That'd be great." They began walking toward the escalator that would take them down to the e-train, which ran between the satellite terminals and the main building of the airport.

"I've cleared the morning for you tomorrow," Kaitlan said. "We can tour the facility then discuss what J. Jacobs can do for your company."

Barbara nodded absently and waited until they were on the train to speak again. She glanced around for a moment then turned to Kaitlan and smiled. "Every time I come into Seattle I like to try and get out for dinner. Don't suppose you'd like to come with me?"

"I - of course, that'd be fine."

"Good." She ran a hand through her hair and turned her attention out the front glass. Kaitlan continued to study her out of the corner of her eye. Barb was a handsome woman and seemed very self-possessed.

As if sensing that she was being looked at, Barb turned and captured Kaitlan's gaze with her own, holding it for a long second while her eyes searched Kaitlan's. Then she grinned, winked, and looked away. Kaitlan, feeling flushed, stared at the floor.

This can't be happening, she told herself. *This woman can't possibly be coming on to me.* Before she had adequate time to consider what Barb was doing, they pulled into the main terminal. Breathing a sigh of relief, Kaitlan followed Barb to the baggage claim area.

* * * * *

After dropping Barbara off at her hotel, Kaitlan returned home to dress for dinner. As she looked through her closet for something to wear, her thoughts returned to Barb's actions at the airport.

What if Barb really were coming on to her? Kaitlan paused to consider how she should react if the issue came up. It had been such a long time since she had made love with a woman, but she wasn't the type to have one night stands.

Then there was the fact that Barbara was a potential client. Kaitlan pulled an outfit out of the closet and started to get dressed while her mind wandered over the potential complications the evening could bring.

Finally, she girded herself to leave, firmly reminding herself that she shouldn't and wouldn't allow herself to be seduced by a good looking woman who might or might not be interested in more than one night of passion.

When Kaitlan returned to the hotel to pick Barbara up for dinner, Barb insisted that she come up to the room while she finished getting ready. Kaitlan sank into a seat in the living room of the suite Barbara had taken and waited while her host finished in the bathroom.

"I took the liberty of making reservations at Chang's Mongolian Grill," Barb called from the other room, startling Kaitlan out of a reverie. "We don't exactly have a wide variety of ethnic food in Juneau." She came out into the main room fastening her earring and Kaitlan had to take a sudden breath.

When she had last seen Barbara, she had looked butch. Now, in a silk blouse and a pair of soft brown leather pants, her shoulder length hair pinned back with combs, she was anything but. Kaitlan blinked twice.

"Is Chang's all right?" Barb asked, smoothing her slacks.

"Fine, it's fine," Kaitlan responded.

Barbara smiled. "Good. After dinner we can stop for drinks."

Thinking that Chang's was located on Capitol Hill, Kaitlan started to ask which bar Barbara liked to go to, but thought better of it. "There are several nice clubs in that area," she settled with.

"I may be mistaken, Kaitlan, but I'm usually not, and I'd guess you're quite familiar with the place I'm talking about. It's on Pike Street."

"Wildrose." Kaitlan felt her stomach twist. "You're talking about Wildrose, aren't you."

"I thought you'd know. I thought so the minute I saw you." Barb was smiling.

"Yes, I know."

"Good. Shall we go?"

VIII.

Five hours later, they were back in Barb's hotel room, sharing drinks and looking out over the city. Kaitlan could feel the vibrations coming from Barb, could almost feel the touch of her fingers on her face. She didn't quite know what to do; she'd never had a female client come on to her before.

"It was a pleasant dinner," Barb said, resting her chin on her fist and looking over at Kaitlan with a faint smile. "I've enjoyed the company."

"Yes," Kaitlan agreed, "it was pleasant." Other than feeling as though Barb had been mentally undressing her for the past five hours, it had been pleasant. It was to the point where despite her earlier promises to herself, the thought of Barb undressing her wasn't exactly unpleasant, either.

"You don't seem like the type to just fall into bed." Barb's words startled Kaitlan so much that she just gaped at the woman opposite her. Barb was studying her glass, then raised her face and tilted it slightly to one side. "That isn't necessarily bad."

"I'm not the type," Kaitlan managed to reply. "I

hope I didn't give you the impression...."

Barb laughed. "No, you didn't give me the impression. I'm afraid I've given you the impression, though."

"Not at all." Kaitlan's voice was weak and she knew it.

"You're very attractive when you blush." Her words were an echo of what Cynthia had said to her that day at the sports club. Kaitlan's face flamed. *Damn! Why did I have to think of Cynthia at a time like this?* Barb must have read her face, because she got quiet for a moment, then said, "Is there someone who might not like me saying that?"

"No. You just - aren't the first person to say it."

Barbara stood up and stretched, then walked over and put her drink on the coffee table near Kaitlan's knee before taking Kaitlan's out of her hand and setting it down.

Dumbly, Kaitlan just watched her as she sank down onto the sofa. Their eyes met. Very deliberately, Barbara leaned over and pressed her mouth against Kaitlan's slightly parted lips, her tongue slipping into the darkness in search of Kaitlan's.

Involuntarily, Kaitlan's arms came up around Barbara's chest. Unable to think under the quiet passion in Barb's kiss, Kaitlan made no protest when Barb pushed her back across the sofa and began unbuttoning her blouse.

Some time later, reason returned to Kaitlan's brain and she broke away from the hungry kiss they were sharing. "Stop," she gasped.

"Why?" Barb's hands were busy somewhere in the vicinity of the buckle to Kaitlan's slacks. She paused long enough to bring one hand up to claim a bare breast. Kaitlan groaned at the darts of arousal that her circling fingers brought on. It had been too long since she felt the touch of another so intimately. Her mind thick, Kaitlan pushed the hand away.

"Just - please, stop."

Breathing heavily, Barbara stopped. She rose up on her hands and knees, frowning. "What's the matter?"

Kaitlan blushed. "I can't do this." She extricated herself from underneath Barb and sat up, looking for her bra. Barb sat back on her heels and stared at her.

"Why not? I thought -"

"I'm sorry, it just isn't - I don't do this."

"You don't sleep with women?" There was a hint of laughter in her voice. Kaitlan frowned.

"I don't have one night stands." The touch on her face was light, then Barb dropped her hand to Kaitlan's thigh where it lay burning her flesh even through her pants. "I should go."

"It doesn't have to be a one night stand. I can stay longer."

Kaitlan located her bra and started to put it on. "Barb, I don't know you well enough."

"What's wrong with good mindless sex? I'm negative." Barb studied her for a moment, gauging her, then kissed her again. This was no tender kiss; her lips pressed hard against Kaitlan's mouth. Her hands became demanding, and again Kaitlan felt her resolve wavering.

"Barbara - please," she tried one last time. But her body was catching the rhythm of Barb's fingers dancing across the fabric of her slacks.

Then suddenly the image of Cynthia's face, turned toward her, her eyes closed, her lips parted, sprang into Kaitlan's mind, the image of Cynthia's face as it had looked after their kiss. She knew that her desire wasn't for the woman next to her, and she couldn't pretend that it was. Abruptly, Kaitlan pushed Barb away and stood up.

"Now what?"

"I'm leaving. I hope you won't let this affect your decision regarding our contract."

Barb crossed her arms. "You don't think this is part of the deal, do you? Because it isn't. It has nothing to do with our meeting tomorrow."

Kaitlan located her bra and blouse and started to dress. "It still isn't kosher. I must look like I'll do anything to land an account."

"Not at all," Barb shook her head. "Really. It's just – we hit it off - and...."

"I'm sorry, Barbara. Maybe I should have one of the other reps sit in on the meeting tomorrow." She went off toward the bathroom to steady herself, her body throbbing and her mind filled with Cynthia.

Barbara called after her, "I want you in the meeting!" Then the phone rang and as Kaitlan went past on her way out the front door, she overheard Barbara talking. "... no, nothing's wrong .... I'm just tired ... Yeah, I miss you, too ... Love you, too ... Oh, I love it when you talk like that."

Feeling slightly ill, Kaitlan pulled the door closed and leaned against it. Then, still fighting the strong ache between her thighs, she pulled out her car keys and headed for the elevator.

*   *   *   *   *

Barbara was already there when Kaitlan arrived the next morning, sitting comfortably in one of the overstuffed chairs in the lobby, sipping on a cappuccino and reading the Wall Street Journal. She was dressed in a conservative business suit, looking nothing at all like either persona Kaitlan had seen the day before.

Barb glanced up when Kaitlan came in and immediately laid down the paper. "Kaitlan!"

Kaitlan flushed. "Ms. Small. Meg, is Cynthia in?"

"Sorry, not yet." Meg handed Kaitlan her mail.

"Thanks. If you'd like to finish your paper, I'm sure Ms. Perry, our Vice President, will be in shortly." Kaitlan started walking quickly toward her office.

"Kaitlan, wait!" Barb was right behind her. "About last night -"

"Meg, hold my calls." Kaitlan led Barb into her office and shut the door firmly. "What do you think you're doing?"

"I wanted to apologize."

"No apology required." Kaitlan crossed to her desk and put her briefcase down, then leaned on her hands and stared down at the polished surface for a brief moment. "You have a girlfriend in Juneau."

"Yes."

"I have never, in my entire life, cheated on anyone. Or with anyone." She turned around and crossed her arms, staring at Barb, who stared back defiantly. "I have always been proud of that fact."

"An admirable quality. Look, Kaitlan, I won't make excuses. I travel a lot, and when I see a good-looking woman like you, I go after her. It's how I am. I'm not sorry for trying."

"I see." They looked at each other in an uncomfortable silence, broken only when Kaitlan saw Cynthia approaching through the glass. "Here's Ms. Perry."

Cynthia rapped, and Kaitlan motioned her inside. "Good morning, Kaitlan," Cynthia said, looking between the two of them.

"Cynthia, this is Ms. Small. Had you arranged a tour for her?"

"Yes. It's a pleasure to meet you, Ms. Small."

"Please, call me Barb." Kaitlan watched the appraising glance sweep over Cynthia's body, then felt a wave of jealousy at the faint smile that appeared on Barb's face. She wondered if Cynthia was the sort Barb would 'go after'. It irked her to think that she might, and irked her even more to think that Cynthia might not turn her down.

"Well, Barb, I hope Kaitlan has treated you well?"

Barb raised and eyebrow and glanced back at Kaitlan, who still stood in front of her desk with her arms crossed. "Oh, quite well. I'm so glad you picked her to represent your company. She's done an outstanding job seeing to my needs."

"I thought you and she would hit it off. Kaitlan, come on into my office in about ten minutes and we'll talk." Kaitlan nodded curtly. "This way, Barb."

Barb stopped at the door and turned back to smile at Kaitlan. "No hard feelings? After all, we will be working together."

Kaitlan, painfully aware of what the lips that were now smiling at her had been doing the previous evening, and of Cynthia's confused expression, forced herself to smile back. "Of course. Enjoy your tour, Barb."

After they were gone, Kaitlan dropped her head and rubbed her temples. So Cynthia had thought they'd hit it off? Just how well did she know Barbara Small?

Abruptly, Kaitlan's head snapped up and she stared after her boss. Cynthia couldn't possibly have set this account up knowing that Barb was a lesbian. Was Cynthia testing her again? Seeing just how far she'd take her vow of non-involvement?

At the end of ten minutes, when she was due in Cynthia's office, Kaitlan had worked herself into a mini-rage. She was convinced that Cynthia had set her up. She was barely able to keep herself in check as she strode through the door at Cynthia's request and positioned herself in front of the big oak desk.

"Well, Barb Small couldn't stop singing your praises, Kaitlan. What'd you do to impress her so much?" Cynthia was smiling.

65

"Do you really want to know?"

Cynthia's smile faded. "What does that mean?"

"Did you think I'd try to sleep my way into an account?"

"What the hell ... what are you talking about?" Cynthia stood up, her brow furrowed.

"How long have you known Barbara was a lesbian?"

Cynthia sat back down suddenly, her face pale. "She's a lesbian?"

"Oh, come off it. You had to know. She started coming on to me before we'd even gotten out of the airport." Kaitlan crossed her arms and stood rock still in front of Cynthia, who was rubbing her neck.

"I didn't know."

"Was this some sort of payback for Friday night?"

Cynthia's head snapped up, lines of anger clearly visible on her face. "No! How dare you even insinuate...." She paused, and looked away. "What happened, Kaitlan? Did you sleep with her?" Her voice sounded tired, as if she didn't want to know the answer.

"I could have. I almost did. I - wanted to."

"What stopped you?"

Kaitlan sighed. "I told you, I don't get involved with co-workers. And I'm not going to sleep with someone just to get their signature on an account."

"I'm hurt that you think I'd set you up like this." Cynthia said, leaning forward. "I wouldn't do that."

"What else was I supposed to think?"

"I had no idea." Kaitlan studied her critically. "I

swear to you, I had no idea. I'd have assigned someone else to the account if I'd even suspected ... I'll put Fred on it."

"No," Kaitlan said slowly, her anger draining out of her. Cynthia looked like she was telling the truth. "No, I can take care of it."

She turned and left Cynthia sitting at her desk with her head in her hands.

IX.

Kaitlan took a sip of her drink and gazed out across the Sound. Below her, she could see Christmas lights on the houses between her and the water. She was glad she had decided to come to the office Christmas party, even if it did mean coming to Cynthia's house.

It was a very nice house, very large. Apparently Cynthia made a good living at her job. The decoration was impeccable, and Cynthia seemed very relaxed in her own environment. Behind Kaitlan, the eddy and flow of conversation in the living room was thinning as people said their good nights. In a few minutes she expected to leave as well. It had been a nice party.

"Here you are." Cynthia's voice was a little tired as she leaned against the deck rail and looked out over the rooftops toward the water. "I've been looking for you."

"I was getting ready to come in and say good night."

"Could I convince you to stay for a little while? I've been wanting to talk with you in private."

Since Barb Small, there had been a degree of tension between them, a tension that had allowed Kaitlan some breathing room and a chance for her desire to cool. As they stood side by side, Kaitlan knew again that it had failed.

"What about?" She tried to keep her tone light, knowing that there were others within hearing range.

"About the SouthAlaska account." Her eyes said there was more, and Kaitlan swallowed, then nodded. Cynthia smiled and went off back into the living room. Kaitlan remained on the deck and finished her drink, listening as one by one, everyone else left.

Finally, she turned away from the view and went back inside. Slowly, she began to gather glasses and ferry them into the kitchen. As she rinsed them and put them in the dishwasher, Cynthia returned from the front door.

"I can do that," she said. "You're a guest."

"I don't mind," Kaitlan replied. "It'll make cleaning up go faster."

Silently, Cynthia started to help her. Once the living room was cleaned up, Cynthia poured Kaitlan another glass of wine and motioned to the couch. "Let's sit down."

They sat for a few moments without speaking, while Cynthia looked out the window. When the silence became unbearable, Kaitlan drew in a breath. "What did you want to talk to me about, Cynthia?"

"You handled things with Barb Small well, Kaitlan."

"I don't think I did." Kaitlan shifted and glanced at the fireplace. "I should never have let things go as far as they did."

"But you must have been tactful about it, because she still gave us the account. I've tried not to question you about it."

"I know. I appreciate that." Kaitlan sighed. Cynthia stood and paced across the room to the bar, poured herself a glass of wine, and turned back.

"But I have to know this. Not as your supervisor. I have to know what stopped you from sleeping with her." Kaitlan started to protest, and Cynthia held up her hand. "Please. My reasons are selfish."

"I - was ready to. But I realized I would have just been using her, that I was thinking about someone else."

"Who?"

Kaitlan considered lying, saying that she had been thinking of Dana, but she couldn't. She swallowed hard and looked into Cynthia's face and answered simply, "You."

Cynthia blushed. "I hadn't dared hope...."

"It doesn't change anything, Cynthia. It doesn't matter that I want you, or how badly I want you. You're still my boss." Kaitlan stood and went to her, longing to hold her, but needing to emphasize that she would not - could not - be swayed.

"It changes things with me." Cynthia sighed. "All my life I've done what I should, what I had to do for my family, my career. The first time I slept with a woman I thought I was being wild, unconventional. Our relationship lasted about a month, and when it was over I realized I had used her almost as much as

70

she used me. But it also made me realize that I couldn't always do what I thought I should."

"What was she like?" Kaitlan thought she could change the subject. Cynthia grinned for a moment, then sobered.

"Kathy Merrill, Captain US Air Force. She was on a TDY here. She taught me things I never knew I could feel. But then she slipped up and I found out she had girlfriends spread across the country. Needless to say, I withdrew from the relationship rather quickly."

"I'm sorry." Cynthia shrugged. "I understand how you feel."

"Yes, well.... I was impressed with you when I found out you hadn't slept with Barb Small. I like a woman who's true to her word."

Kaitlan didn't answer her, and they stood in silence for a few seconds. Then Cynthia stood on tiptoe and kissed Kaitlan on the cheek, startling her. "Why'd you do that?"

"Because. I guess it was sort of a good bye."

"Good bye?" Kaitlan frowned. "What do you mean?"

"I mean, I've got to get over this problem I have with you, and I might as well start now."

Kaitlan looked down at her, at the warmth in her face, at the strain hiding just below the surface. She felt a wash of desire, of wanting to comfort and love the woman next to her. Cynthia returned the gaze, neither breaking away.

Then Kaitlan kissed her. As she felt the melting lips against hers, she realized that she had known all along she would do this, would give herself to this dark woman.

They stood in the living room, just their lips touching, for what seemed an eternity. Finally, Cynthia stepped away, breathing raggedly. "Kaitlan...."

"Cynthia. Put your wine down." Cynthia turned and obeyed slowly, and Kaitlan came up behind her. Burying her face in the thick black hair, she breathed the scent of Cynthia's shampoo.

"Kaitlan," Cynthia repeated, turning into her arms. "Oh, Kaitlan."

"I've been so stubborn," Kaitlan whispered, kissing her forehead. "I've tried so hard, and all this time I've been involved. I've been involved since the first time you walked into my office."

"You have no idea...." Their second kiss was mutual, hungry. Kaitlan's hands trailed up Cynthia's sides, seeking the softness of her breasts through the silk blouse. She felt Cynthia shudder and moved her fingers down along the planes of her back to cup her hips, pulling her closer.

"Come upstairs with me." Cynthia stepped back and took her hand. Kaitlan allowed herself to be led up the stairs and down the hall.

In the doorway of what could only be her bedroom, Cynthia stopped. "I don't want you to do this if you have any doubts," she said. In response, Kaitlan swept her into her arms and stepped into the room.

"I have no doubts." She kissed Cynthia again, her hands coming to the buttons on the blouse. She trembled as the fabric parted beneath her fingers, desire swelling within her until she felt ready to burst.

Finally, the garment hung open and Kaitlan slid it off Cynthia's shoulders, leaving her in her slacks and a lacy black bra through which her nipples could just be seen.

"Close the door," Cynthia whispered. Kaitlan complied, then took Cynthia's hand and led her to the high queen-sized bed. They looked at each other for a long, simmering moment. Then Kaitlan pressed her lips to Cynthia's, gently lowering her to the coverlet.

Her hands were sure now, unfastening the black lace and pulling the bra off. She rose up and gazed down on Cynthia's breasts, heaving in erratic time with her breathing. "You're beautiful."

Cynthia's response was to wrap her legs around Kaitlan's waist and draw her in, her hands busy pulling the shirt over Kaitlan's head. Kaitlan helped shrug her bra off, then pressed against Cynthia, groaning softly as she felt the hardness of Cynthia's nipples against her skin.

They kissed deeply, tongues dancing in sweet darkness, then Kaitlan lifted herself enough to unfasten the belt to Cynthia's slacks. Cynthia lifted her hips as Kaitlan pulled the pants down. She glanced up and drew in a sharp breath as she saw the briefs Cynthia wore, high cut and matching her bra. Only a thin line of a scar just above the waistband marred the silky darkness of her skin. Cynthia's hands were running across her shoulders. Her voice, when she spoke, held the barest hint of a laugh.

"Something wrong, Kaitlan?"

"No," Kaitlan managed, finding her throat suddenly dry. Deliberately, she kissed up the inside of one thigh and snapped at the elastic of the briefs with her teeth. Cynthia gasped, then let out a low groan. "Something wrong?"

"You're such a tease," Cynthia replied as Kaitlan began to move across the fabric, nuzzling into it and breathing deeply of Cynthia's scent. Slowly, Kaitlan pulled the briefs down, her eyes on the thick triangle of black hair revealed beneath. She stood long enough to get out of her own trousers, then stepped between Cynthia's legs and lay down, pulling Cynthia fully onto the bed beside her.

"You have the most beautiful body." Kaitlan whispered into her ear before kissing her passionately. Cynthia's response in her arms told her that Cynthia had no doubts as to what she was doing.

Kaitlan raised a hand and traced one small breast, her fingers lightly caressing the hardened nipple. Cynthia moaned softly, closing her eyes. Smiling to herself, Kaitlan bent and ran her lips across both breasts, then took a nipple into her mouth and began to suck at it. Her hand now ran down between Cynthia's legs, teasing, exploring. She found Cynthia wet and brought her hand up to taste that wetness on her fingers.

Cynthia murmured something and pushed at her head, guiding her down her body. Kaitlan willingly nestled between her legs, her lips moving through the tangle of hair as she sought to draw the essence of

74

Cynthia into her soul. Cynthia bent her legs, lifting her hips. "Please...."

Slowly, Kaitlan spread Cynthia with her fingers. Then, taken by a desire unlike anything she had ever experienced, she dropped her head, claiming the darker woman with a hunger that threatened to overwhelm her. Cynthia's back arched and she let out a single gasping cry, then her hands wove into Kaitlan's hair.

Kaitlan explored her with long, eager strokes, sliding her hands under her buttocks to lift her against her mouth. Her tongue flicked at the hardness of Cynthia's center, then she drew it between her lips and sucked at it. Cynthia groaned, a long, impassioned plea for release, but Kaitlan wasn't ready to let her go. She began once again to explore, delving inside Cynthia's warmth and tasting all of her.

"God, Kaitlan, please.... Oh, please, don't stop. Just like that." Cynthia's voice was hoarse with desire. "God, I've wanted this for so long...."

And then there was no holding her back as she exploded into orgasm. Kaitlan felt the spasms coming and pressed her lips against her, taking the pleasure as it flowed from her, until finally all that remained was a small tremor in her thighs. Kaitlan kissed the top of her curls, just below the scar, then moved up her body to take her in her arms.

"Thank you," Cynthia whispered, curling against her. "You have no idea –"

"Ssssh. Relax." Kaitlan stopped her as her hand began to delve between Kaitlan's legs. "We have all night together."

"But I want...."

"There's plenty of time." Kaitlan kissed her softly. "Don't think I'm through with you yet."

They rested for a few minutes, then Kaitlan didn't stop Cynthia as she turned to her, her hands exploring, her mouth hungry. She felt Cynthia's hair falling across her chest as the darker woman suckled at her breast, and wondered that she could be so excited by the touch of someone. It was an exquisite agony of desire that tormented her until Cynthia's mouth moved further down her body, until Cynthia showed her that she did, in fact, know how to please a woman.

X.

Kaitlan shifted and felt the warm arm across her waist tighten, pulling her back into an embrace. Startled into full wakefulness, she stared into the dim morning light at an unfamiliar room. A moment later, the scent of Cynthia's perfume came wafting to her, and she remembered.

With remembering came desire, and so Kaitlan rolled over to kiss her companion awake. Looking down on Cynthia's face, relaxed in sleep, Kaitlan felt a surge of love that almost frightened her. Unable to stand watching the peacefulness, unable to handle her own emotions, she bent her head and kissed Cynthia on the mouth.

"Good morning," she whispered when her eyes met Cynthia's. Cynthia's lips curled into a smile.

"It is, isn't it?" She drew Kaitlan down into another longer kiss that turned passionate. Kaitlan felt the swelling ache between her legs, and moved her hand to see if Cynthia was experiencing the same hunger.

Her fingers found wet and warmth, and she began to move them while her mouth sought out a nipple to suckle. Cynthia groaned and wove her hands into

Kaitlan's hair. A moment later, Kaitlan moved between her thighs, pulling her to her knees as her fingers slipped inside. Again she bent her head to suckle at Cynthia's swollen breasts. Cynthia's nails clawed at her back as she moved against Kaitlan's hand and moaned her hunger.

The sound of the door swinging open came to Kaitlan's ears a second too late. Too startled to react in any other way, she turned to see who was coming into the room. "Holy shit! Mom!"

The girl, perhaps twenty, stood in the doorway, frozen with one hand on the knob, her jaw hanging slack. Kaitlan glanced at Cynthia, and found a similar expression of shock on her face. The two stared at each other for a long second, then the girl flushed beet red and retreated.

"Oh, Christ," Cynthia whispered. "I was so close ... I didn't hear ... I didn't think...."

"Who was that?" Kaitlan withdrew her hand.

"Ginny. My daughter. She's home for Christmas break. Oh, my god."

"She doesn't know?" *Christ, you knew she had children.*

"No. I have to talk to her - before she calls her father...."

Cynthia got up and pulled on her robe. Hastily, Kaitlan got dressed and the pair went down the hall to Ginny's room. It was empty. Downstairs, they heard the sound of the TV.

Ginny sat on the couch, her eyes glued to the screen, watching an infomercial. She didn't move

when Cynthia and Kaitlan came in. "Ginny, honey...,"
Cynthia began, then trailed off. Ginny turned,
blushed, and dropped her eyes.

"I'm sorry, mom, I should have knocked."

"Yes, I guess you should have. Uh, I know you
must be very confused right now."

Ginny shook her head, and then nodded. She
glanced at Kaitlan and narrowed her eyes. "I know
you must be older than you look," she said, "but you
don't look old enough to be my step-mother." Kaitlan
blushed.

"I should have told you children, I knew I should
have said something sooner." Cynthia paced. "Ginny,
sweetheart, what did you see?"

Ginny swallowed. "I saw enough. You know, it's
hard enough imagining your mother having sex with
your father, but to see her with another woman...."

"This is probably coming a little late, dear, but I'm a
lesbian."

"I gathered that," Ginny responded dryly. "Look, if
you're going to have girlfriends over, I wish you'd
warn us not to come barging in."

"This wasn't exactly planned," Kaitlan interjected.
Ginny turned at looked at her again.

"Are you saying my mother is a one night stand?
Because if you are I'll pop you one."

"No, no ... I'm just saying neither of us intended for
me to stay the night. Look, I'd better leave, Cynthia.
I'll talk to you tomorrow at the office."

"Kaitlan, please." Cynthia held out her hands.
"Don't rush off."

Kaitlan felt a sudden rush of embarrassment. Not at what had just happened, but at what had happened the previous night. She had given in despite all her vows to the contrary. And despite the dull ache that persisted in her body even now, she felt the need to escape.

"I - I have to go. I'm sorry, Cynthia, I really am, I just...." Unable to explain, Kaitlan grabbed for her purse and coat and made a line for the door. Cynthia followed her.

"What's the problem? Kaitlan - what's wrong?"

"I can't talk about it - I'm sorry. I'm so sorry this happened - I never intended -" Cynthia reached out to touch her and she evaded the fingers, remembering all too well what they had done to her the night before.

Cynthia looked hurt. "Kaitlan, please. Don't do this."

"I – God, I'm so sorry." Kaitlan pushed out the door and almost ran to her car, fumbling for her keys. She knew Cynthia was standing in the doorway watching her, but she didn't dare turn back. She had to escape, had to flee from the emotions that coursed through her and made her want nothing more than to return to Cynthia's arms.

The car jerked as she put it in gear, then she took off and headed home, trying to catch her breath and her sense of reason. When she finally turned into the parking garage, she had her breath back, but not her reason. She felt disoriented, as if she were underwater and unable to find the surface.

The phone was ringing when she opened her door.

She crossed the room and stood by it until the answering machine picked up. Cynthia's voice came over the speaker, sounding urgent.

"Kaitlan - please pick up if you're there. Please. What the hell is going on? Ginny's okay with things. It's no big deal. I thought we were past all this. Kaitlan, call me. As soon as you hear this."

There was a click and the machine beeped. Kaitlan stood staring at it, struggling with herself. Twice she reached for the phone, and twice pulled back. Finally, she spun and crossed to the bar and poured herself a stiff drink.

The phone rang again. "Hi! It's Lynda. Where are you?"

Kaitlan grabbed the phone and waited for the machine to cut off. "Lynda. I need to talk to you."

"Where the heck have you been? I've been trying to reach you since eight last night!"

"Can you come over? Now?"

Lynda paused, and Kaitlan listened as she conferred with Alex. "Yeah, I can swing by. What's wrong?"

"I'm in trouble. Serious trouble."

Lynda's voice grew worried. "What happened?"

"I've made a huge mistake. I don't want to talk about it on the phone." Kaitlan took a swallow of her drink and coughed as the alcohol burned down her throat.

"I'm on my way." The phone clicked and Kaitlan replaced the receiver before pacing toward the window. Unbidden, images of the previous night filled her thoughts. She shuddered at the memory of Cynthia's skin so smooth beneath her fingers, at the look of ecstasy on Cynthia's face as she had arched up from the bed in orgasm, at the angelic innocence on that same face in sleep. Groaning, Kaitlan drained her drink and fixed another.

Finally, the doorbell rang. Relieved, she went to open the door. Lynda came inside and looked around, then looked at the glass in Kaitlan's hand. "This doesn't look good."

"Lynda - I've really screwed up."

"You look like you slept in that outfit. Is there any coffee?"

Kaitlan glanced helplessly at the kitchen. "No. I only just got home half an hour ago."

Lynda stopped halfway to the kitchen. "Got home? Where were you?"

"Cynthia Perry gave an office party last night."

"You didn't." Kaitlan nodded miserably. "You did. Oh, shit, Kaitlan. Were you drunk?"

Kaitlan threw her a dirty look. "I don't get drunk. You know that."

"Was she drunk?" Kaitlan shook her head. "So ... this was a mutually agreeable thing?"

"I shouldn't have - I didn't mean to - it just ... happened." She sank down onto the sofa and Lynda joined her.

"You mean you gave in. She wasn't happy about it this morning?"

Kaitlan stared at the ceiling and tried to collect her thoughts. "She thought it was wonderful. So did I, until her daughter walked in on us."

Lynda stifled a laugh. "She did what?"

"It isn't funny. We were - involved at the time."
Lynda burst out laughing. "It isn't funny!"

"Yes, it is."

"I'm not ready for this," Kaitlan muttered, dropping her head. "I'm not ready to get involved with someone. Especially not Cynthia Perry."

"Why not? She's smart, she's attractive, and she makes a lot more money than you do."

"Damn it, Lynda, I thought you'd understand." Kaitlan set her drink down forcefully and ran her hands through her hair. "She's my boss. I'm breaking my number one rule. This can't work out."

"Kaitlan, you're overwrought. Calm down and think about this. It's hardly a sin." Kaitlan snorted. "It isn't."

Kaitlan started to respond, but was interrupted by the sound of the doorbell. Frowning, she got up and crossed the room and looked through the peephole. "Shit," she whispered. The bell rang again.

"Aren't you going to answer it?"

"It's her." Lynda rolled her eyes and motioned for her to open the door. Steeling herself, she did.

Cynthia looked disheveled, as if she had just thrown on clothes and dashed out the door. Even so, Kaitlan was swept by a surge of emotion so close to love that it made her dizzy. She reached for the doorframe to support herself.

"Kaitlan - we need to talk."

"What are you doing here? I'm not ready to talk to

you." Her voice was as weak as her knees.

"Oh, for Christ's sake, Kaitlan, let the woman in." Lynda sounded imperious. Slowly, Kaitlan stepped back to allow Cynthia inside. Cynthia saw Lynda and drew up short.

"I didn't know you had company. She is company, isn't she?"

"Yes, I'm company," Lynda said, smiling. "Company who is just leaving."

"Lynda -" Lynda held up her hand and Kaitlan fell silent.

"I'll talk to you later." Kaitlan watched Lynda stroll out the door, and then turned to look at Cynthia.

"What happened, Kaitlan?" Cynthia asked, her voice weary.

"I made a mistake, that's what happened. Last night - was a mistake." Kaitlan hoped her voice was stronger than she felt. Cynthia frowned.

"Why was it a mistake? Why?"

"I can't be involved with you. The problems at work...."

"There won't be any problems at work."

Kaitlan sighed and ran a hand through her hair. "Oh? And what happens when someone figures out that we're sleeping together? Someone like Patsy?"

Cynthia let out a long breath and bit her lip. "I hadn't thought about that."

"You may not realize this, but Patsy does not like me one bit. I don't think she'd pause two seconds before using this against me."

"But, Kaitlan, I don't know if I can forget what

happened last night. It was ... more than I ever thought it could be."

Kaitlan paused, studying Cynthia's face intently. Finally, she pursed her lips. She couldn't waver, couldn't give in. She knew what she had to do. "I'm sorry, Cynthia. But there can't be anything between us. I won't allow it."

"If you're sure that's the way you want it...." Cynthia looked disappointed.

"I'm sure. I'm sorry if I hurt you in any way - "

"No, no I'm not hurt." Her face told a different story, but Kaitlan forced herself not to react. Turning, Cynthia put her hand on the doorknob. "I'll talk to you tomorrow."

After she had gone, Kaitlan stared at the door, her glass in her hand. Finally, shaking herself and taking a drink, she sank down onto the sofa and closed her eyes against the unexpected tears that formed there.

XI.

"Meg, could you come into my office for a minute?" Kaitlan motioned at the secretary as she strode past. Meg followed, closing the door behind her.

"What do you need, Ms. Davis?"

"I just got a call from Peyton-Smith. Did I or did I not ask you to fax a set of estimates to them two days ago?"

Meg frowned. "Well, yes. And I did. I can get the log."

"No, no." Kaitlan shook her head. "They got the estimates. But I don't think the set you sent was the set I asked you to send. They've basically said there's no way in hell they'll do business with us. What did you send them?"

"I sent the contents of the file you gave me," Meg responded, looking white.

"They also claim I called them and tried to bully them into placing an order at an outrageous markup." Kaitlan was fuming. She knew fully well she hadn't made any such call, and she had a suspicion who had. "Did you leave that file on your desk?"

"Well, yes, I did. When I went to lunch. I don't see...." Meg looked upset. "I'm sorry if I sent the wrong thing."

"It's not your fault, Meg. I'm sorry if I sound angry, but any minute I'm going to get my butt hauled into Cynthia's office for a royal ass-chewing and I haven't got a clue what's going on."

"Well, Patsy dropped something off for me to send right after you did, maybe you should ask her if she saw anything."

"I might just do that." Kaitlan stood up to let Meg out and saw Cynthia standing in her doorway. Her heart leapt as it always did, despite her best efforts. It had been five long, tense days of tight silence between them and Kaitlan was feeling the effects. She could still remember Cynthia's voice screaming her name in the throes of ecstasy, and it was hard to accept the strained silence that followed their conversation afterwards.

Cynthia saw her and motioned her, then turned and vanished into her office without waiting for Kaitlan to get there. Sighing, Kaitlan stepped inside, knowing what was coming. She expected it would be worse because of the current tension between them.

"Close the door." Kaitlan complied and crossed the room to sit in one of the armchairs in front of the desk. Cynthia templed her fingers and stared at them for a moment before speaking. "I've spoken to Mr. Heinz just now. He's furious."

Kaitlan groaned inwardly. Mr. Heinz was the president of J. Jacobs. The people at Peyton-Smith must have been angrier than she thought. "I didn't make that call."

Cynthia sighed. "I'm sure you didn't. The question is, who did?"

"You want my opinion?" Kaitlan raised an eyebrow. She hadn't expected this. "Patsy is the only person in the office who could impersonate me on the phone."

"Can you prove she cocked up this account? If you can, I'll have her ass."

"I can't prove anything. But I didn't do it. I know that. I can show you my paperwork."

"Kaitlan, I believe you. But Heinz wants your butt in a sling. I've managed to put him off for the moment. But there's only one way out of this mess."

"That is?" For a split second, Kaitlan wondered if Cynthia could have screwed the account up as payback. As soon as she thought it, she was embarrassed. Cynthia was many things, but vindictive didn't seem to be one of them.

"I spoke to the president of Peyton-Smith. They're willing to give us one more chance. But you and I are going to have to come up with a damn good proposal for them or they're taking their account elsewhere. I hope you don't have plans this weekend."

The two women studied one another. Kaitlan saw the unspoken words in Cynthia's eyes. *Don't worry*, they said. But Kaitlan worried anyway. "I suppose you could come over this evening and work."

"My house is closer."

Kaitlan cleared her throat. "I'd rather not ... it

would feel awkward."

"Okay," Cynthia sighed, closing her eyes for a second. "Your place then. Kaitlan, we've got to at least be able to speak to each other. I won't mention it if you won't."

"Deal." Kaitlan stood up. "I promise, we'll knock out the best proposal Peyton-Smith has ever gotten."

Cynthia smiled tightly. "I'm sure we will."

On the way back to her office, Kaitlan ran into Patsy. The bespectacled woman jumped slightly when she saw Kaitlan standing there. "Oh! Hello, Kaitlan. So sorry to hear about the Peyton-Smith account."

"I'll bet," Kaitlan responded archly. "Who told you?"

"Uh, you know how the office grapevine works." Patsy's eyes darted nervously around the room. Then she seemed to get herself under control. "Better be careful. Mr. Heinz doesn't appreciate screw-ups in major accounts. I don't care how much Cynthia likes you, she won't be able to protect you if Heinz decides to drop you."

"What's that supposed to mean?" Kaitlan frowned.

"Oh, I think you know what I mean. Just be careful."

"No, Patsy, I think you'd better be careful. Someone else screwed that account up, and if I find out who it was, they're going to be sorry."

"You'd never be able to prove it. Might as well just take responsibility and hope for the best. Now, if you'll excuse me...." Patsy strode off, leaving Kaitlan red-faced and ready to explode. Finally, she turned and walked into her office to try and sort the mess out.

*   *   *   *   *

Kaitlan pushed her laptop away from her and rubbed her eyes. Across the table, Cynthia was looking equally tired.

"I'm starved," Kaitlan groaned.

"So am I. Shall we order something?"

Kaitlan laughed. "No, I can throw something together. I don't much call for cooking lately, but I enjoy it." She got up and went into the kitchen. After a moment, Cynthia followed her. "Do you like chicken?"

"Yes. Can I help?" Kaitlan shook her head and Cynthia leaned against the counter to watch her preparing the meal. She pulled chicken breasts from the freezer and put them in the microwave on defrost, then retrieved fresh vegetables from the refrigerator and started chopping them.

"I'll throw together a chicken pasta primavera. There's a bottle of Chianti on the top of the wine rack, why don't you open that?"

Cynthia moved to get the wine, then started rummaging around for an opener. She finally located it and popped the cork, then pushed the bottle back to breathe. "You seem to know your way around a kitchen," she commented as Kaitlan deftly minced garlic to add to the olive oil she had started in a skillet on the stove.

"I love to cook. Dana and I used to have a lot of dinner parties. I'd even make the hors d'ouevres. She made the drinks and played host. The perfect couple." Kaitlan was surprised at the bitterness in her voice. To herself, she muttered, "what a joke."

Cynthia was silent for a moment, then shifted and made a noise in her throat. "She must have hurt you terribly when she left."

"You could say that." Kaitlan forced herself to keep calm as she sliced the chicken and added it to the pan. "She took everything but my clothes."

"That might explain it then."

"Explain what?" She looked up from stirring. Cynthia shrugged.

"Why you won't let me in," she said simply, then walked back into the dining room. Kaitlan could see her working on the proposal again. With a sigh, she swallowed the urge to forget dinner altogether and started the pasta.

When she sat the plates down on the table, Cynthia was printing out the last pages of their work. She went back for the wine and as an afterthought grabbed the lighter to light the candles. Cynthia cleared away their work and the two sat down to eat.

"I'm sorry I said that earlier," Cynthia said softly a while later. "I had no business to."

"It's ok," Kaitlan replied. "You could even be right."

"Are you really happy with the way your life is turning out?"

Startled, Kaitlan looked at her across the table. The

glow from the candles cast moving highlights into Cynthia's hair. Sighing, she dropped her gaze to her plate. "Not particularly."

"I'm sorry if I'm being overly persistent," Cynthia replied. "But I - that night was something I can't just forget."

"What about your children? You seemed awfully concerned that Ginny might call your ex-." Kaitlan toyed with her pasta.

Cynthia was silent for a moment. "I was. That was a shortcoming on my part. I've talked to Ginny and Terry. I even offered to pay for counseling for them." Kaitlan couldn't help the snicker that escaped her lips and Cynthia looked sharply at her for a moment. "So I'm old fashioned."

"Well, what did they say?"

"Ginny rolled her eyes and told me to grow up and Terry kept asking if I was going to get a crew cut and pierce something." Kaitlan raised an eyebrow and Cynthia shrugged. "He's eighteen. But actually, I guess I raised them up all right because they were both mostly concerned with whether I was happy or not."

"Well, considering the scene the other morning, I'd say Ginny is going to – what did she say – pop me one? If she ever sees me again." Kaitlan managed to smile. Cynthia laughed.

"I talked her out of it. I told her that whom I saw was really my own concern and I didn't want her threatening my dates. Actually, I'm glad I've talked with them. I was getting tired of always trying to arrange to meet people somewhere else."

Kaitlan poured two more glasses of wine and pondered Cynthia's words. They finished their meal and moved to the living room. When Cynthia sat down on the couch, Kaitlan paused a moment before sitting beside her. Cynthia sighed and leaned her head against Kaitlan's shoulder. Silence reigned for a few minutes.

"You have no idea how I wish this were all less complicated," Kaitlan said finally.

"It's obvious you're attracted to me," Cynthia replied. "And I'm attracted to you. Patsy Frasier be damned. I think we should leave work out of it for once."

"I do want you, you know that. But ... I don't even really know why I'm trying to keep you at arms length."

"Kaitlan, this come here – go away attitude is very hard for me to handle. I need to know where I stand with you."

Kaitlan lifted a hand to brush through Cynthia's soft black hair. "I've wanted to be with you from the first time I saw you, even when I thought you were straight. But I have this fear ... you can't imagine the damage Dana did to my psyche. Not only that, but you're everything I always swore I'd never become involved with ... newly out, with children, my boss ... when I think about it, my head aches. It aches almost as much as my body does when I look at you."

"That doesn't answer my question." Cynthia looked serious.

"No, I don't guess it does." Kaitlan sighed. "I guess that if I'm to be involved with you I have to be willing to open myself up to the hurt that could result."

Cynthia pulled away and stood up angrily. "So that's all I represent, you possibly getting hurt?"

"No!" Kaitlan gasped, horrified that she had been misunderstood. "God, no."

"Then make yourself clear, damn it!"

"Cynthia, I want you. More than I've ever wanted anyone."

"But?" Cynthia crossed her arms.

Kaitlan looked at her for a long moment, and then admitted what she had been trying to keep from even herself. "I'm afraid."

The dark haired woman stared at her. "You're afraid? Of what, me?"

"I'm not sure."

Cynthia glanced away, then back at her. Silence reigned for the space of time it took for her to cross the distance to the sofa, then she took Kaitlan's face in her hands and kissed her.

It was a long, slow, gentle kiss, her tongue making lazy circles around Kaitlan's lips, dipping inside ever so briefly to dance against Kaitlan's. Kaitlan sat still, unsure of how to respond, wanting desperately to take Cynthia in her arms but not sure if it would be welcomed.

Then Cynthia stepped back and looked down at her. "You have no reason to be afraid of me, Kaitlan."

"I don't want to be."

Cynthia took her hands and pulled slightly. Kaitlan stood silently. Cynthia reached up to caress her cheek. "I want to make love with you, Kaitlan. Let me."

Looking into her eyes, Kaitlan felt her fears begin to dissolve. Here was a woman who knew what she wanted, who was patiently asking for something she shouldn't have to ask for. Cynthia would be the one to lead the way, and Kaitlan was ready to let her.

"Come with me." Kaitlan squeezed Cynthia's hands, then dropped one and led her by the other down the hallway to her bedroom. Cynthia pushed the door closed as they entered, then stepped in front of Kaitlan.

"Let me show you how I feel about you. Let me show you that you don't have to fear me." Her fingers were on the top button of Kaitlan's shirt. Dumbly, Kaitlan nodded.

Slowly, Cynthia unbuttoned the blouse, then pulled it away from her shoulders and slid it down her arms. Kaitlan stood still, feeling the softness of Cynthia's fingers as they caressed their way up her arms to her neck. Ever so slowly, Cynthia moved her hands into Kaitlan's hair and pulled her head down. They kissed with agonizing slowness while Cynthia unfastened Kaitlan's bra and pulled it off.

Her hands came to cup Kaitlan's breasts, fingers exploring the curves and lines of her, the palms of her hands moving in small circles over the hard buds of her nipples. Kaitlan groaned when fingers, sure and knowledgeable, closed around her nipples and

95

pinched lightly.

"I do know what to do with a woman," Cynthia breathed into her mouth.

"I guess you do," Kaitlan murmured back, raising her hands to Cynthia's waist. She pulled the silk blouse out of Cynthia's slacks and began unfastening it even as Cynthia bent to take a nipple in her mouth. She drew it between her teeth and flicked it with her tongue.

Kaitlan felt her knees weakening. It was as if Cynthia sensed this, as she backed Kaitlan to the bed and pushed her gently down across it, coming on top of her without releasing her lips from the breast she suckled at.

Warmth flooded Kaitlan's belly and spilled down her legs as they parted to allow Cynthia to kneel between them, her mouth moving down Kaitlan's body, her hands busy at the buckle of her belt. Her mouth left Kaitlan only long enough for her to pull her trousers and underwear down, then she was kissing up the inside of one thigh with whispering kisses.

Kaitlan tried to speak and failed. She couldn't remember the last time she had been seduced so well. She had always been the one to initiate lovemaking, had always been in control. But abandoning that control the Cynthia was the easiest thing in the world. Kaitlan started to puzzle over it, but when Cynthia's breath stirred the thatch of hair at the top of her thigh, conscious thought left her.

Cynthia's tongue ran a lazy line down toward the

hottest part of Kaitlan's body, found and claimed her center with a suddenly sure stroke. Kaitlan arched her back and gasped aloud as Cynthia's mouth fastened against her. Then there was only the melting pleasure that the strokes of her tongue brought.

When the blinding crash of light and sensation hit her, Kaitlan found herself crying Cynthia's name aloud, her hands tangling in the thick black hair. Then as the orgasm faded, she found herself simply crying with the knowledge that she had almost lost Cynthia forever, had almost never allowed herself to know what depth of emotion Cynthia was capable of.

Cynthia came into her arms and kissed away her tears, murmuring reassurances as Kaitlan tearfully whispered "I'm sorry," over and over. She held the woman close to her, wanting to fix the feeling of her supple body in her thoughts forever.

Finally, the tears slowed, and Kaitlan reached for a tissue. Cynthia rolled over and sat up, unbuttoning her blouse the rest of the way.

"I'm so sorry for crying," Kaitlan said ruefully. "I don't know what came over me."

"I understand. I don't mind, really."

"I should be doing that," Kaitlan protested as Cynthia stood and shrugged out of the rest of her clothes.

"Not tonight. Tonight you're going to let me erase all thoughts of anyone else from your mind." Naked, Cynthia crawled back onto the bed and into Kaitlan's arms. "You have goose bumps. Let's get under the covers."

Once they were comfortably ensconced beneath the blankets, Cynthia turned to her and kissed her softly. Kaitlan sighed her pleasure as she felt the warmth of skin pressed against her, then Cynthia slid a thigh across hers and moved on top of her again.

It was much, much later that they finally fell asleep enfolded in each other's arms.

XII.

Sunlight filtering through the blinds woke Kaitlan the next morning. She felt Cynthia's body next to her, listened for a moment to the regular sound of her breathing, then looked up at the ceiling and smiled.

Moving slowly so as not to awaken her companion, Kaitlan slipped out of bed and padded toward the kitchen to start coffee and breakfast. As she ground beans and measured the water, her mind replayed the previous night in glorious detail.

She found the bed tray and set up two cups of coffee and plates with cheese Danish and fruit, then returned to the bedroom. Cynthia had rolled over onto her back, her head to one side, one fist tucked under her chin. Kaitlan stopped and looked at her, struck once again with the beauty of the woman sleeping her bed.

As she stood in the doorway, Cynthia stirred and opened her eyes. She focused on Kaitlan and smiled. "Good morning."

"Good morning. I made breakfast."

"Mmm." Cynthia stretched. "I can think of something else I'd rather have first."

"The coffee will get cold," Kaitlan protested with a laugh. "And it's fresh ground, too."

"All right, then." Cynthia made room as Kaitlan carefully climbed onto the bed and sat the tray down. She handed Cynthia one of the coffee mugs and took one herself. "I'd better get a kiss before you start drinking."

Kaitlan willingly kissed her, wishing she could keep the feeling of those lips with her all the time. Finally, Cynthia sat back and took a sip of her coffee.

"Thank you for last night," Kaitlan said softly. "I've been a real jerk and I know it."

"Yes, you have been. But I knew I could get to the real you if I tried hard enough." Cynthia quirked her mouth into a grin.

"You surprised me. I didn't expect...." Kaitlan trailed off, blushing.

"What, me to be aggressive?"

"Until last night I thought of you as so many things, but never as simply a woman I wanted to be with. I let all the trappings get in the way of realizing you were not all that different from me."

Cynthia laughed. "You mean a woman who has a terrible case of the wants? I know; you seemed shocked that I knew what I was doing."

"Well, you hadn't really said you had much experience." Kaitlan wished her face would stop turning red.

"I have more than you might expect, darling."

"Mmm, I like it when you call me darling." Kaitlan smiled with the memory of the previous night.

Cynthia had called her darling frequently.

"Does that mean you aren't going to run screaming again?" Kaitlan nodded. "Good. I was getting very tired of chasing you."

"I'm caught."

"You know, if you feed me a grape, I might let myself get caught too." Laughing, Kaitlan complied.

A while later, the tray having been moved to the floor to prevent it from being knocked over, the two women lay side by side looking into each other's eyes. "What would you like to do today," Kaitlan asked, running her fingers up one firm thigh.

"Wander down to Pike Street and see what's fresh?" Cynthia smiled. "Although you seem to be rather fresh this morning."

"I see my cooking has impressed you," Kaitlan replied with a little laugh. Cynthia nodded. "OK, Pike Street it is then."

"At some point I need to feed the dog. And get a change of clothes. I don't feel like wandering around on a Saturday in my business suit."

"I wish you didn't live so far away." Kaitlan bit her tongue as soon as she spoke. "I mean – it'll be inconvenient to go all the way to Redmond and come back just for dinner."

Cynthia leaned over and kissed her. "I wasn't planning on coming back just for dinner. I have a lot of making up to do with you."

"Well then, we might as well start now." Kaitlan pulled her close and kissed her.

Their coffee was very cold by the time they got out of bed.

*　*　*　*　*

"Ms. Davis, Ms. Perry needs to see you in her office as soon as you get a moment."

Kaitlan looked up from her desk and nodded. "Thank you, Meg."

She closed her file and stood, trying to keep her steps sedate as she crossed to Cynthia's door. Out of the corner of her eye, she saw Patsy standing in her own doorway watching her intently.

Resisting the urge to lift a finger at her, Kaitlan instead rapped at Cynthia's door and listened for the voice to tell her to come in. When it came, she slipped inside and shut the door behind her.

"Meg said you needed to see me?" Kaitlan forced herself to stay on her side of the desk as Cynthia looked up and smiled privately.

"Yes. Our proposal was accepted by Peyton-Smith. I guess all that hard work paid off."

"That's a relief. I'm sure Patsy will be spitting nails when she finds out though." Kaitlan ran through a litany against Patsy in her mind.

Cynthia stood and came around to her, stepping carefully into her arms and kissing her with a soft determination that left Kaitlan breathless. "Yes, darling," she whispered. "But if Patsy hadn't screwed things up we wouldn't be where we are now."

"Cynthia ... God, you smell good." Cynthia

102

smiled. "But don't you think it's a bad idea for us to do this at work?"

"I suppose you're right," Cynthia sighed, stepping away. "I just miss you during the day. I miss being able to kiss you whenever I feel like it. And I hate not being able to grab that cute ass when you walk by me."

"You grab my ass in public and we'll both be looking for new jobs," Kaitlan said severely. Then she laughed. "Although it might just give Patsy a heart attack."

It was Thursday. Kaitlan had spent the previous three nights at Cynthia's house. With the ice broken, their relationship had begun to build a foundation that was beginning to look more solid than even the one she and Dana had shared.

She had discovered that Cynthia had a passion for art, as did she, and that they held similar tastes in music, wine, and literature. It had been a moment of amazed laughter between them when they discovered that they both harbored deep secret crushes on the young Katherine Hepburn and a taste for caviar right from the jar.

"I don't want to talk about Patsy any more. I do have to maintain my impartiality at work, darling." Cynthia went back to her desk. "Are we still meeting your friends tonight for dinner?"

"Yes, at seven. You remember Alex and Lynda – I was with them that night on the cruise."

"That's right, Alex is the lawyer who works for the LRC." Cynthia shuffled some papers on her desk.

"Are you almost done with your work? I thought maybe...." She glanced through her lashes at Kaitlan. "I thought maybe you could help me move something at home before we head north."

Kaitlan laughed. "Sweetheart, I'd move the sky for you, you know that."

"I was thinking more about the earth." Cynthia wiggled her eyebrows lecherously. "And I know you can do that quite well. So? Are you done?"

"Give me five minutes."

*   *   *   *   *

They were late meeting Alex and Lynda at the restaurant. Lynda took one look at the pair as they dashed in and started laughing.

"What's so funny?" Kaitlan demanded as she pulled out the chair for Cynthia. Lynda shook her head and kept laughing. "What?"

"You two. Even if you weren't still grinning like fools ... it isn't like you to be late, Kaitlan. And good thing you showed up, you're starting to look pretty thin. Don't you guys ever eat?"

Kaitlan glanced over at Cynthia and blushed. "We - uh.... Don't be such an ass, Lynda. At least let me introduce you properly before you start with the rude comments."

"Take all the fun out of it, why don't you?" Lynda grinned, then subsided. "Nice to officially meet you, Cynthia."

"You too. Kaitlan is always going on about the two

of you." Cynthia looked over at Kaitlan. "When she isn't busy, that is."

"God, two of you," Kaitlan groaned. "Alex, save me, I think these two have the same sense of humor."

Alex giggled and reached for her wine. "Hey, leave me out of this."

They paused in their ribbing to order drinks, then conversation turned to the LRC.

"Alex was telling me they lost their head of fundraising last week. Too bad you couldn't apply for that one, Kaitlan." Lynda reached over and took her lover's hand. "Of course, I'm not sure I'd want you hanging around my girl all day."

"I have my hands full enough as it is," Kaitlan replied.

"How is that working, the two of you in the same office?" Alex asked. "I would think, from a legal standpoint ... aren't you having trouble with someone you supervise, Kait?"

Kaitlan considered her comment. "I had been trying not to think about that. It's something we haven't really discussed yet." She glanced at Cynthia, who looked up from the menu and smiled softly. "I do like my job, but...."

"We have time to think about it, dearest," Cynthia said in a quiet voice. "Patsy will be too busy cooking up some other scheme to notice anything odd for a while yet."

"Speaking of odd," Lynda broke in. "Guess who called me yesterday looking for you, Kaitlan?"

"Who?" Kaitlan slid her hand onto Cynthia's thigh

under the table.

"Dana."

Cynthia jumped as Kaitlan's fingers tightened. She forced herself to relax and took a drink of wine before answering. "Why is she looking for me? I have nothing to say to her."

"I guess things are going kind of rough at work. She sounded pretty frazzled. Said she was beginning to think she had made a mistake."

Kaitlan's voice was hard. "Did you tell her to go to hell?" Cynthia's hand covered hers under the table and squeezed.

"No. I didn't give her your number, either. Though she asked for it. Twice." Lynda ran her finger around the rim of her water glass for a moment. "I think she's losing it. She's been in teen-crisis counseling too long."

"I couldn't care less if she ran naked down Broadway," Kaitlan growled. "Let's just drop the subject."

"What looks good to you, Cynthia?" Alex interceded and deftly turned the conversation into safer waters.

XIII.

The next two months passed for Kaitlan in a blur of happiness. While she and Cynthia still maintained their separate houses, they often slept at Cynthia's during the week and Kaitlan's on the weekend. This Friday night, she was cooking dinner while Cynthia finished getting ready for a play they were attending later that evening. It was a domestic setting; one Kaitlan treasured more with each passing day.

Dinner was almost done when the doorbell rang. Kaitlan could hear the shower still running, telling her that Cynthia wouldn't be able to answer it. Grumbling, she pulled the pan she was sautéing in off the burner and went to see who it was, fully expecting to find her neighbor in need of something minor. She pulled open the door and stared at the visitor.

"Hello, Kaitlan." Dana walked past her into the apartment as though she had simply forgotten her key. Dazed, Kaitlan turned and followed her, closing the door. "Nice little place you've pulled together."

"What the Hell are you doing here?"

"I came to find you. You know I still love you."

Dana's gaze traveled around the living room to the two briefcases on the sofa. "Who's here?"

"Dana, you have some goddamned nerve –" Kaitlan fumbled for words to express her outrage.

Dana sighed. "I was going through a rough time. I did some stupid things. But I'm better now, and I still want to be with you."

Kaitlan managed a weak laugh. "You call cleaning out our house a 'stupid thing'? You call sleeping with my best friend a 'stupid thing'? I'll tell you what's stupid, Dana. Thinking I would take you back after what you did to me."

"Every relationship has its rough times, sweetheart...."

Kaitlan was very glad that Cynthia chose that moment to walk into the room. She was toweling her hair and stopped to look quizzically at the newcomer.

"I didn't hear the door," she commented. "Unexpected dinner company?"

"No." Kaitlan glared at Dana, who was appraising Cynthia with a critical and extremely jealous look on her face. "I think she's just leaving."

"So, Miss Moral High Ground ... the minute a crack shows you're ready to throw away twelve years without a second thought, eh?" The snide tone in Dana's voice brought Kaitlan's anger to a bubbling head.

"I did no such thing, Dana. I'd say moving to Arizona is slightly more than a crack. Or should I quote that damned letter you wrote me?"

Cynthia, realizing who Dana was, stepped closer to

Kaitlan. "Should I go, Kaitlan?"

Kaitlan put a hand on her arm to reassure her. "No. Dana is the one who will be going. I don't know how you tracked me down, Dana, or what insane idea you've got in your head, but we are through. We've been through for over a year. So go home to Rebecca and leave me alone."

Dana's face contorted in anger. "I'm not giving up that easily, Kaitlan. We spent too many good years building our relationship to let it just evaporate." She turned on Cynthia with venom in her voice. "I will fight for what's mine. I know Kaitlan better than any person alive. She belongs with me. I don't know who you think you are, but –"

Cynthia's voice as she interrupted was cool and deathly serious. "I'm the woman who loves her. Really loves her. I don't want to own her like you do. But I can assure you I am not someone you want to screw around with. Now, I believe Kaitlan asked you to leave."

Dana paused a moment as if considering another attack, then pulled back. "Fine. But this isn't over by any means, Kaitlan. Don't forget what I said in that letter. I love you. I will always love you."

With every ounce of dignity Kaitlan could muster, she reached for the doorknob and pulled. "Get out."

As the door closed behind Dana, Kaitlan let out a long breath. "Jesus."

"Where did she come from?" Cynthia was still eyeing the doorway uncertainly. "And what kind of drugs is she on?"

"I don't know.   Damn it, dinner is probably ruined."   Cynthia moved to wrap her arms around Kaitlan as her shoulders heaved. "I'm not crying."

"I know."

"I can't believe after all this time … she actually thought I'd take her back."   Kaitlan felt comforted by Cynthia's embrace and bent to kiss her forehead. "I wouldn't, even if I hadn't met you."

"I'm not sure how to take that," Cynthia teased, lifted her face for another light kiss. "After all, I just professed my undying love for you."

"Yes, you did," Kaitlan replied seriously. "I didn't expect it."

"I hope it doesn't scare you. I don't want to own you. Just to love you."   Cynthia rested her head against Kaitlan's chest. "And maybe someday to have you love me back."

A lump rose in Kaitlan's throat as she felt Cynthia against her. Her voice sounded strange to her ears as she spoke. "I do love you. More than I ever thought I could love someone again."

"You do? But you haven't…."

"I've been so afraid of my own damn shadow I haven't been able to think clearly."

Cynthia sighed contentedly. "I never expected my life to turn out like this, but I certainly can't complain."

"I'm glad to hear that," Kaitlan laughed. "Now, why don't you open some wine and I'll try to salvage dinner and let's see if we can forget Dana Mitchum ever existed."

*   *   *   *   *

Kaitlan was going over the weekly reports when she heard Meg's voice through the open door of her office mention her name. Glancing up, her jaw dropped. Dana was standing at the reception desk. "Shit," she murmured to herself.

Moving as quickly as she could without drawing attention, she crossed the open waiting area, praying that she could get Dana outside before she opened her mouth. Dana saw her and met her halfway. "I told you we weren't through discussing things, Kaitlan."

"Dana, you can't just show up at my workplace and expect me to be able to talk."

"You won't answer your phone." Dana crossed her arms.

"Fine, come into my office." Kaitlan turned and started to walk back toward her office.

"Why, so no one else hears what a slut you are?" Dana's voice was loud enough to attract attention from other people in the room. Out of the corner of her eye, Kaitlan saw Meg pick up the phone.

"Please, come into my office, Dana." She tried to control her voice, to keep it low. "We can talk there."

"No. I think I want this to be nice and public. You won't answer your phone, you delete my email, you act like I don't exist. Guess what, Kaitlan. I do exist, and I'm not going away." Dana jabbed her finger at Kaitlan, who bit her lip and struggled for a graceful way out of the situation.

111

"Everything that needed saying has been said. Now if you don't calm down, I'm going to have to call security."

Dana reached out and slapped her. "Bitch. If you think I'm going to let some little chippie come between you and me, you're sadly mistaken."

Dazed, Kaitlan stared at her, her hand going to her cheek. "You hit me! Have you lost your fucking mind?"

"I love you, Kaitlan. And you love me, or you said you did. You can't make that go away."

Jesus Christ. Kaitlan felt her world spinning away from her as she realized that by now everyone in the office was watching them. "Are you trying to get me fired?" She hissed. "Lower your voice."

"Oh, so you're back in the closet now?" Dana's face contorted into a sick grin as she spoke even more loudly. "No one knows you're a dyke?"

Trying to regain control of the situation, Kaitlan forced her expression to sink into calmness. "Well, I guess they all do now, don't they, Dana? You've made your little scene, I suggest you leave before security throws you out."

"What is going on out here?" Over Dana's shoulder, Kaitlan saw Cynthia come out of her office.

Oh no, can this get any worse? Kaitlan tried to flash a warning sign but Cynthia saw Dana and strode over. Dana turned as she approached. "You."

"Yes, me. What are you doing here? Meg, call security."

"I already have, Ms. Perry."

"This is a secure building, Ms. Mitchum. You're going to find yourself in a lot of trouble if you don't leave immediately." Cynthia crossed her arms and scowled at the intruder. Dana read the brass plate on the door of Cynthia's office and laughed.

"So, you're Kaitlan's boss then. Is that it, Kaitlan? I didn't make enough money for you so you moved in on someone who did?"

"Dana, shut up. You're the one who left me, remember? I don't know what you're expecting to gain by this little show, but there is no way in hell I would take you back. Not if you were the last person on earth." Kaitlan's voice was a harsh, loud whisper. "And don't you dare make any assumptions about my relationship with Cynthia."

"But you are sleeping with her. Or is she in the habit of showering at other people's apartments?" Dana's face was red. "And does your boss usually announce that she's in love with you to perfect strangers?"

Cynthia put her hand up over her face and made a sound that could have either been disgust or frustration. Behind her, two security men came into the room. Kaitlan looked once more at the woman she had wasted so much time pining over and felt nothing but anger. "Your escort has arrived Dana. Now get out and I don't ever want to see you again. Ever."

"Ma'am, will you come with us?" One of the guards put his hand on Dana's arm.

"I will never forgive you for this, Kaitlan. But I will still always love you." Turning, Dana allowed herself to be led away.

Kaitlan blew out a long breath and forced herself to look around the room. Everyone ducked back into their offices as her gaze neared them, but when her eyes met Patsy Frasier's and all she could see glittering in them was triumph.

XIV.

"Well, this is just a total disaster," Cynthia said as she took a long drink of wine. Kaitlan shifted her gaze from the ferry lights out on the Sound to her companion and nodded silently. "We could both get fired, you realize this."

"I know. I am so sorry, Cyn –"

"Don't be. There's nothing to be done about it now. But what will we do? Damn, I've spent twenty years getting where I am in that company." She leaned forward in her chair and rested her forehead against the deck railing for a moment. Behind them, in the house, Ginny was watching TV.

Kaitlan shrugged. "Well, there is that position at the LRC. I'm pretty sure I could get it with my experience. Of course, you have more experience than I do."

Cynthia laughed, a strained sound. "Maybe I should go to law school. My father is a lawyer, you know."

"No, I didn't. Mine is an auto mechanic. But he likes it. I grew up in a pretty small town. My mom was town clerk for a few years."

"Do they know...?" Cynthia looked at her curiously. "I haven't even thought of what to say to mine."

"Yes, they know. We don't really talk about it." Kaitlan looked back out over the water and sipped her wine. "I love you."

"And I love you. We'll be fine, one way or the other." Cynthia leaned over and kissed her softly.

"Mmmmm," Kaitlan sighed. "Be careful, I'm not so distracted you can't get in trouble with kisses like that."

"Maybe I'm trying to get into trouble." Cynthia ran light fingers up Kaitlan's thigh and kissed her again, more firmly.

"Ginny's home," Kaitlan protested weakly. "Remember what happened last time."

"I'll lock the door, I promise." Cynthia raised her eyebrows. "Are you turning me down?"

"You, my dear, are incorrigible."

*   *   *   *   *

Kaitlan looked up from her work as Cynthia came into the office. The look on her face said it all. "We've been called up," she commented. "You might want to start thinking whether you want a blindfold or not."

"Let's just get this over with," Kaitlan replied, standing. She smoothed her skirt and took a deep breath before joining Cynthia. The two of them walked slowly down the hall to Mr. Heinz's office. Cynthia took her hand and gave it a quick squeeze

116

before pushing the door open and stepping inside.

The secretary looked up, saw them. "They'll be with you in a moment."

A few minutes later the door to the inner office opened and Patsy Frasier stormed out. She shot the pair a venomous look before stalking from the room. Trying to keep her face a calm as Cynthia's, Kaitlan ushered Cynthia in through the open door. The man behind the massive desk stood as the two women entered.

"Cynthia, Ms. Davis, come in." Kaitlan noticed that there were two other men already present. Inwardly, she groaned. "Cynthia, you know Dan Williams, VP of Personnel. And this is John Rollins, our lawyer."

Cynthia inclined her head to the two men. Mr. Heinz gestured to two empty chairs in front of the desk, and Kaitlan sank into one, grateful for the support of the seat. Cynthia took the other and shot her a wan smile.

"Cynthia, we've been made aware of the incident that occurred in your division two days ago," Dan Williams began. "You know we strongly disapprove of office romances, and to have something like this happen ... well, it just doesn't make anyone look good."

"I'm aware of that, Dan," Cynthia replied. "The situation got out of control through no fault of Ms. Davis', however." Kaitlan noticed she didn't respond to the mention of an office romance.

"Ms. Davis ... your name was associated with a foul-up in one of our major accounts just recently, was it not?" Dan shifted his attention to Kaitlan.

"Yes, Sir," she said weakly. "But Cynthia ... Ms. Perry and I resolved the difficulty."

"How long have you worked here, Ms. Davis?"

"Six months, Sir." Kaitlan saw her career vanishing quickly. "But Ms. Perry really wasn't involved in the scene the other day ... it was my fault."

"You are involved in a romantic relationship with each other, are you not?" Mr. Heinz spoke, looking between the two of them.

Cynthia answered in a voice that was probably stronger than she felt. "Yes, we are. I'm aware that office policy discourages intra-office dating, but...." She trailed off.

John Rollins spoke next. "It seems our guidelines for office conduct are somewhat vague. Apparently, we give the impression that we discriminate on the basis of sexual orientation. I'm here to reassure you that this company has never and will never do so. Certain persons from your office came to us in the apparent hope that your relationship was cause for your termination."

"Patsy," Kaitlan muttered under her breath.

"When Mrs. Frasier came to us with this information, we took it upon ourselves to look back over your record, Ms. Davis. And upon some research, we determined which extension was used in making the call to Peyton-Smith which resulted in their almost canceling their contracts with us."

"I can assure you Kaitlan was not responsible – " Cynthia began.

"The call came from Mrs. Frasier's office," Mr. Heinz said calmly. "Since it seems apparent that Mrs. Frasier is willing to sacrifice the good name of this company in order to fulfill some personal vendetta against you, Ms. Davis, she has been told that it would be best for her to seek another position."

Kaitlan and Cynthia exchanged startled glances. "But...."

"Now, as to the scene the other day. Can we be assured that sort of thing won't happen again?" Dan asked casually.

"Certainly!" Cynthia looked shocked. "But ... I thought ... I was sure...." Again she trailed off and looked confused.

Mr. Heinz smiled. "Cynthia, you've been with us for over twenty years. We can't afford to lose your experience."

"However," John added. "You can see the difficult situation we are in, considering that you both hold management positions in the same department. You are open to charges of nepotism."

"Sir, with all due respect," Kaitlan said. "I have been considering resigning for just that reason." She glanced at Cynthia, who smiled softly. "We didn't mean for all of this to happen. If you would just give me two weeks to find another position...."

"We would hate to lose you," Dan replied. "Your sales numbers are strong. But I think considering the situation it would be for the best. We will, of course, give you an excellent reference."

"Thank you."

119

Mr. Heinz rose. "Well, now that that is taken care of ... I have some other things to attend to." Cynthia and Kaitlan also got up and shook the hands of the men in the room before leaving. Once in the hallway, Cynthia turned to Kaitlan with a look of shock on her face.

"Did what I think just happened really happen," she asked dazedly.

"I think so," Kaitlan replied.

"I think this calls for a celebration!"

"I'll get my coat." Kaitlan laughed. "We can buy a bottle of champagne and take the afternoon off!"

Cynthia gave her a look that sent a shiver down her spine. "Only if we can drink the champagne in bed."

"Last one to their car buys." Giggling, the two women started off at a quick trot for their office.

*   *   *   *   *

"Well, I'm glad that's over." Kaitlan looked over her shoulder as Cynthia joined her on the deck. She held out a glass of wine. "You weren't kidding when you said you loved to give parties."

"I tried to warn you," Kaitlan laughed, taking the wine. "Next time we throw a fundraiser, we'll get a restaurant. Is everyone gone?"

"Alex and Lynda are in the kitchen. Doing dishes supposedly. You know," Cynthia leaned against the railing beside her. "You seem to be doing a hell of a job at the LRC. Alex keeps going on about you."

"She's my friend, she has to. How is William

working out?" William Flint had been tapped to fill Kaitlan's position when she resigned to take the fundraising job at the LRC.

"Just fine." They stood together, looking out over the water, not speaking for a space of time. "Did I ever tell you how good you look in a tux?" Cynthia asked finally, turning to her.

Kaitlan lifted her free hand to trace her fingers along the bare line of Cynthia's shoulder. "You look stunning in that dress," she replied. "I thought so the first time you wore it."

"God, that dinner cruise. I'm glad we've progressed from that point.

"Me, too." Kaitlan put her arm around Cynthia's waist and drew her into an embrace. They kissed deeply, then Cynthia rested her head against Kaitlan's chest, her arms around her.

A discreet cough broke them apart some time later. Lynda was standing in the doorway to the living room, holding her coat. "We're leaving, guys. Great party."

"Thanks, Lyn." Kaitlan walked over to give her friend a hug. "And thanks for the info on Dana. I was afraid she was being so quiet because she was plotting something."

"No," Lynda laughed. "I called Rebecca as soon as I found out about her little scene and told her to come get the bitch. I guess Rebecca had been looking all over for her. She must've really gone off the deep end."

"You could say that," Kaitlan replied dryly.

"Well, she's in a good hospital, from what I hear. I just can't believe Rebecca would take her back after all she pulled."

Kaitlan shrugged. "It's over. Let's forget about it. You and Alex have a good time this weekend."

"We will." Lynda leered and winked. "I'm sure you will too."

"Get out of here, you bum."

After walking Lynda and Alex to the door and locking up behind them, Kaitlan returned to the living room, where Cynthia sat on the loveseat waiting for her.

"Ready for bed, beautiful?"

"Of course. I'll need help out of this dress, though." Cynthia looked up at her through her eyelashes and smiled slyly.

"Are the kids coming home?" Kaitlan couldn't help but grin at the blush that ran up Cynthia's face.

"Wench. I'll get you for that." Kaitlan was two steps ahead of her as they ran up the stairs. Inside the master bedroom, she caught Cynthia around the waist and pulled her into a tight embrace, kissing her passionately.

"Now, about that dress?"

Later, comfortably ensconced under the covers, Cynthia curled into Kaitlan's arms and sighed in satisfaction. "I do love you."

"Oh, yeah? Prove it." Kaitlan gave her a steamy look. Cynthia reached up and lightly pinched one nipple, laughing when Kaitlan jumped.

"I intend to." And she did.

Publications available from
Cape Winds Press, Inc.
PO Box 730428   Ormond Beach, FL 32173-0428
Web Site: http://www.capewindspress.com

We welcome mail orders. Please add 15% for shipping.

TAHOMA by M. Broughton Boone, 165 pp. Can two women find happiness in the Washington Territory of 1883?   ISBN 0-9671203-0-6 $12.95

A WILD SEA by Rebecca Montague, 174 pp. A ghost from the past threatens to destroy a present love.
                    ISBN 0-9671203-2-2 $12.95

ALLERGIC REACTION by Leslie Adams, 151 pp. First in the Debutante Detective series. A country club beauty with a secret distracts detective Porter Sienna during a murder investigation.
                    ISBN 0-9671203-3-0 $11.95

OFFICE HOURS by M. Broughton Boone, 122 pp. A Cape Winds Weekend Escape. Will Kaitlan Davis break her number one rule and get involved with her boss?   ISBN 0-9671203-4-9 $10.95

Printed in the United States
1463600001B/286-291